T5-BCL-804

UNDERNEATH THE WATER WITH THE FISH

Copyright © 2020 Carol Malyon

Except for the use of short passages for review purposes, no part of this book may be reproduced, in part or in whole, or transmitted in any form or by any means, electronically or mechanically, including photocopying, recording, or any information or storage retrieval system, without prior permission in writing from the publisher or a licence from the Canadian Copyright Collective Agency (Access Copyright).

We gratefully acknowledge the support of the Canada Council for the Arts and the Ontario Arts Council for our publishing program. We also acknowledge the financial support of the Government of Canada.

Cover design: Val Fullard

Library and Archives Canada Cataloguing in Publication

Title: Underneath the water with the fish : stories / Carol Malyon.
Names: Malyon, Carol, 1933– author.
Series: Inanna poetry & fiction series.
Description: Series statement: Inanna poetry & fiction series
Identifiers: Canadiana (print) 20200208195 | Canadiana (ebook) 20200208209 | ISBN 9781771337496 (softcover) | ISBN 9781771337502 (epub) | ISBN 9781771337519 (Kindle) | ISBN 9781771337526 (pdf)
Classification: LCC PS8576.A5364 U53 2020 | DDC C813/.54—dc23

Printed and bound in Canada
Inanna Publications and Education Inc.
210 Founders College, York University
4700 Keele Street, Toronto, Ontario M3J 1P3 Canada
Telephone: (416) 736-5356 Fax (416) 736-5765
Email: inanna.publications@inanna.ca Website: www.inanna.ca

UNDERNEATH THE WATER WITH THE FISH

SHORT FICTION

CAROL MALYON

inanna poetry & fiction series

INANNA PUBLICATIONS AND EDUCATION INC.
TORONTO, CANADA

*This book would have been dedicated
to Else Shimrat;
it's dedicated to her memory instead.*

ALSO BY CAROL MALYON

POETRY
Headstand (1990)
Emma's Dead (1992)
Colville's People (2002)

SHORT FICTION
The Edge of the World (1991)
Lovers and Other Strangers (1996)

NOVELS
If I Knew I'd Tell You (1993)
The Adultery Handbook (1999)
The Migration of Butterflies (2004)
Cathedral Women (2006)

CHILDREN' BOOKS
Mixed-up Grandmas (1998)

NON-FICTION
griddle talk (co-written with bill bissett) (2009)

Table of Contents

TABLE OF CONTENTS

Bad Men Who Love Jesus
at the Last Minute

D ADDY WAS ALREADY SIXTY-SEVEN before he decided to give his soul to the Lord. Lucky for him that God's so patient. He'd been a rotter all his life, then suddenly he turned into someone I'd read about in the Bible and heard about in Sunday sermons: that prodigal son.

Sixty-seven plus eleven months to be exact, and not likely to make it to sixty-eight. "I saw the dazzling light last night, Kiddo," he told me. "I had a vision, just like Joan of Arc. Those saints and holy martyrs have them all the time. I saw Jesus walking toward me, just ambling along. Why would He bother hurrying anyway? Time means nothing to Him. Ain't that right? We were far off in some empty desert, nothing else in sight, not even a camel or cactus plant. That's how come I could see Him from so far away. I didn't know who it was at first, just some guy in a white bathrobe, and wearing sandals, casual, like swimming pool thongs. When He got close I knew I'd seen Him some place before, maybe in some bar or donut shop. But then I remembered all those churches with stained-glass windows. Dammit, I was scared shitless; you better believe it. I was pretty sure my time had come. So I flopped down on the burning hot sand and touched the hem of His dusty bathrobe. Somebody did that in the Bible, so it seemed like a good idea."

I started shaking, my teeth kept chattering. "Oh no!" was all I could say.

Daddy rambled on, looking smug. "It was so hot. Sweat was dripping into my eyes. I guess that's why I didn't recognize Him at first. It was hot like you can't imagine. My clothes were soaking wet with sweat. I told Him I had a couple of regrets. I don't, but it seemed like something He'd wanta hear."

"But you're old now, Daddy. You're ancient. How come you waited so long to get religion?" I had to holler because he can't hear so good.

"I don't know, Kiddo. I just kept putting it off until next year and then the next. But last night I was feeling so poorly. Suddenly I knew I'd better hurry up. I hadn't much time."

It isn't fair.

That old bastard will be on his way to glory, his elbow nudging open that heavenly gate. St. Peter will try to slam it shut but Daddy will shove his foot inside, like when he was still a door-to-door salesman and selling vacuum cleaners to gullible housewives.

Will he see Baby Alice up there? Will they have to be united again? My little sister that he shook senseless? Will he be able to shake her again? Poor sweet innocent Baby Alice. I sure hope not.

And what about Momma? All her bruises must be faded by now. Will Daddy start bashing her again?

"The Lord doesn't stock any shelves with liquor," I hollered. "Bet you didn't think about that." My daddy's been a mean drunk ever since I can remember. He can't ever keep a job because of sneaking a mickey inside his lunch pail.

Daddy started laughing. "Guess I'll have to find out where they stash the communion wine. Heh, heh, heh." But then that laugh turned into a cough.

"Take those words back," I hollered. "Tell Jesus you were kidding. Say you changed your mind. Heaven is supposed to be beautiful. I don't want you up there staggering around, vomiting your guts out, smashing dishes and knick-knacks, messing up the place."

I hate listening when Daddy hacks like that. Finally, when he got his breath back, he scrunched his eyes shut and pretended to be asleep.

I kept hollering at him anyway. "Damn you, Daddy. Wake up and tell Jesus you made a mistake. You've been a sinner all your life. A no-good rotter. It's way too late to change." I dared to say this because I felt safe inside that hospital ward, and anyway he was too sick to chase me. "You've been a low-down weasel ever since I can remember. Beating us kids with your belt until we were bleeding. Always cheating on Momma. Fucking every woman in sight. Babysitters and neighbours, even me, your only daughter. You've been a bad man all your life. Don't chicken out now. Don't pray for forgiveness at the last minute."

At least we live in Canada. In the U.S. they think beating your wife and family is nothing. When a man hurts a woman, it's just a big joke. It happens all the time in the movies and on TV. Examples ought to be made. Then maybe the men would stop.

Why don't churches do something about it? Why didn't Momma? Why doesn't God?

Daddy sneaking into my bedroom at night. How come Momma didn't pay attention to that? Didn't she notice? Didn't she care? Maybe she was just glad he wasn't bothering her.

She always said I was making up stories. She wouldn't notice a lamp post if she bumped her head against it. No light bulbs clicking on inside her brain like happens in comic strips.

My own Momma thinking I must be crazy. I'd be listening to my Walkman, laughing sometimes, and she thought I was hearing voices. That woman. What can you do with someone like that? I mean, I loved her. She was my Momma after all. Every Christmas I bought her a present. Also birthdays. And a fancy card on Mother's Day with a gushy verse and pictures of pink flowers. I always smoked my cigarettes outside, but all that's not good enough.

She paid a doctor ten dollars to break into my room and say

I was crazy. That way he could fill me up with drugs,giving me bad trips with sleeping pills or placebos or something. Trying to murder my brain. Doctors! They've got no right to do that. They act like veterinarians. I'M A PERSON!

Some people take drugs and others don't. I don't want any chemicals messing up my head.

Those doctors sniffed cocaine and then stuck poison needles inside me. They tried to numb me into a zombie. They do whatever they want. They want me to just sit still like a lamp post or flowerpot. I need some civil rights.

I started hollering at Daddy again but he didn't even bother to answer, so I unfastened that plastic oxygen tent. I grabbed hold of his shoulders and shook him. "Listen here, old geezer. Pay attention to what I'm saying! This is important!"

But a buzzer was making too much of a racket and a bunch of people started running around in the room. They shoved me out into the hall, but I pushed right back in again, and hollered, "Watch it. I belong here. I'm the daughter." Someone stuck a big needle into Daddy. Somebody else was pounding his chest.

I started yelling, "Oh no! Is he trying to die? Oh no!"

And I yelled at Daddy. "Don't do it, Daddy. Don't go yet. Don't head for that dazzling tunnel that leads straight into heaven. Stop! Don't go zooming along it."

Then they wheeled in an electric machine. Some nurse grabbed me and turned my head so I couldn't watch. She hugged me so hard it hurt, and then shoved me down on the floor. "Kneel and pray for your daddy's soul," she said. "He's on his way to meet the Lord."

So I started screeching. "Watch out, St. Peter. If you let Daddy inside heaven you'll be sorry. He'll wreck the place. You'd better fasten the deadbolt and put a chain on the door. Hang a NO VACANCY sign outside. Just yell at him through the keyhole to go away. To take a flying leap and land in hell where he belongs."

But I already knew it was too late. God damn it.

A nurse held me tight and said it's all over. "Your daddy's gone to be in paradise with God and the angels."

I'll have to learn to shoplift. I'll knock over sweet little old ladies and steal their purses. "Sorry," I'll tell them. "I've got no choice. But be careful landing. Don't break your hip."

I'm going to have to learn to shoot dope and striptease and lap dance.

I don't want to do those things, but I'll have to. No way I'm going to end up in the same place as my dad.

In Bed Beside a Stranger

ANNIE WAKES UP BESIDE A STRANGER and wonders why this always happens. Perhaps this is a man she has been dreaming of, buying clothes to be noticed by, getting a different hairstyle so he will want to run his fingers through it. "It's so soft," he will say, meaning her, meaning her hair, her lips, her nipples, the pink petals he unfolds between her legs. This man she thinks up witty comments for, trying to impress, and gets off the bus three stops too soon hoping to run into, invents reasons to call up on the phone, hoping this time he will recognize her voice, remember her name.

Perhaps she wakes up beside someone she's been living with for a week, a month, a year. Annie can't be sure of the time because the person in her bed seems to keep changing.

Anyway, this seems fair, because every morning she wakes up a different person than whoever she was the day before. She thinks this is because she always wakes up beside a stranger. She thinks that this makes sense.

Annie checks her daughter's photograph to see whether the stranger in her bed bears a family resemblance. She could phone her mother to make sure her stepfather isn't missing. Doesn't she have a stepfather? She isn't sure.

She calls friends, neighbours, women from work, but no one seems to know who she went to bed with the night before. Annie wants to warn them to check their beds for strangers but hates to alarm them. Anyway, they will notice soon enough.

A stranger slumbers beneath the quilt her mother-in-law stitched when her son and Annie got married; that nice woman Annie can hardly remember, though she still sleeps beneath that quilt. The son thought he knew what he was doing and handed Annie a ring; she thought she did too, so she took it. And all his mother could do about it was stitch a quilt, with scraps left over from making flowered aprons. A double wedding ring design. Interlocking rings that Annie hardly noticed at first, then tried to get used to, but finally couldn't bear to look at because men hate seeing women cry.

It is some sort of family tradition to give this quilt to couples. They'll stay together so long as they never get out of bed.

Annie is used to the interlocking rings by now and hardly notices them at all, but she notices the stranger underneath them.

The stranger could be dangerous. Annie reads of so many weirdos in the newspaper and hears about them on the news, and never feels sympathetic. How could that woman have let a stranger into her house? Her bed? Her body? This is the kind of thing Annie always wonders.

As though there comes a moment when men stop being strangers. When it is safe for a woman to open up her house, her bed, her life. A time to cover the man with a quilt, rings interlocked on top, the man and woman interlocked underneath. As though there's a time when it's all right, and women have some way of knowing when.

She wants to phone a lost and found to inquire about missing persons; if no one matches the stranger's description she could report a found person, but they would probably assume she was joking and hang up.

She could phone the police department, but she knows he didn't break in: no windows are smashed; two wine glasses are on the bedside table, and the stranger's hands are not the part of him that makes her nervous. Even though she can feel his fingerprints all over her body, and knows that if a detective placed her under ultraviolet light they would show up everywhere. There is no part of her body his hands haven't touched. She is conscious of the feel of them, like semen on her thighs, like a memory almost forgotten, like a feeling she washes away, then wants right back.

Annie wakes up beside a stranger. This sometimes happens. She doesn't know what to do about it, so she touches him anyway.

Bruise-Woman

B RUISE-WOMAN WEARS DARK GLASSES, talks to herself. "I know Mort really loves me. He just can't bring himself to say it. His momma never taught him loving words. Anyway, he knows I'll always be here, like a table or bed or sofa. He can come home and kick his shoes off, relax, watch TV wrestling, do whatever he wants. Can drink one beer and then keep drinking. He works hard. He's entitled.

"Next day he always begs me to forgive him, he never meant that slap to happen. And I tell him it's okay; it was my fault. I shouldn't have made him mad."

Amanda has never known her father, so Mort thinks he has the right to give her advice. He thinks he has that power, even though she loathes him and he knows it. The advice always happens just as the police discover his whereabouts and he disappears again.

"Pay attention, girlie. This is important. You can't trust people. Especially politicians. Don't trust them or anyone else. Politicians just do whatever they want and charge us taxes to pay their big salaries. We keep paying and paying. They let lots of people come into this country. They want more people so they can get more taxes.

"A lot of those strangers aren't even legal. If they get caught and put in jail, what do they care? Jail is probably better than life wherever they came from. Trust me. I've been in jail and I know. Life isn't so bad. You live inside a building, not in a doorway or on top of a sewer grating. You're warm and dry, not getting snowed or rained on. You sleep in a bed and eat three squares a day. Why wouldn't deadbeats be happy to get put inside a jail?

"They take our jobs and paycheques. And we folks who belong here can't find a job, so why should we even bother to look. We can't pay our rent and don't know where to turn or what to do.

"Those illegals are everywhere, and I can't even understand what they say. And they don't understand me either. They say their English isn't good enough. But that's not my fault, is it?

"People always do that, try to shift the blame on you, as though everything is your fault. Don't let them get away with that. Fight back. Don't give an inch.

"When my grandma and grandpa came to this country, things were a whole lot different.

"Say no to immigration as soon as you're old enough to vote. Say no to welfare and subsidized housing, things the rest of us have to work hard for. People ought to pay their own way. Otherwise they won't bother working at all.

"Don't forget this, girlie. Because I won't be here when you're grown-up. I'm not going to stick around much longer. One of these days I'll wave bye-bye to your Momma and catch a Greyhound bus headed for somewhere else.

"You don't think I'm good enough for your Momma, but just you wait. She'll cry her eyes out when she finds out I've flown the coop. Gone forever. You'll miss me, too. Who else is gonna teach you what the world is really like? All the bad stuff you've got to watch out for? Not your Momma. She lives inside some dream world. She still believes those sweet little fairy tales someone read her when she was a kid. They were just stories but your Momma never figured that out. Someone got paid good money for making them up."

Amanda is talking to herself, wishing she could confide in someone.

Momma knows her place. Beside the stove or ironing board or washing machine. Handy. Mort always knows where to find her, to beat her up whenever he feels like. Who's strong enough to stop him? Not Momma. Not me, scrawny little two-bit kid.

No place where we could hide out, relax, and feel safe. Well, it turned out there was a shelter, but we didn't know that then. Later on we found it.

Mort acting as though he owned her, like a puppy with a choke chain on its neck that the owner can yank whenever he feels like.

Bad day selling used cars? Come on home, Mort. Knock Momma around. Maybe her black eye will make you feel better. Upset about gambling debts, pot belly, balding head? Shove Momma against the counter, slap her, spatter a pattern of her bright red blood on the kitchen floor.

Sometimes I visit classmates after school, dawdling, delaying as long as I can, but finally having to go home. I tell Momma things that surprise her: "Hey Momma. Guess what? Mr. Simmons kisses his wife," and, "Mr. Barton reads stories to his kids."

Finally Mort shoved her once too often. A broken rib flattened her lung the same way a nail punctures a tire. A doctor called the police and that was that.

Poor sweet Momma kept feeling guilty, saying, "It wasn't his fault, Amanda. I deserved it. Men get angry if supper's not ready on time. It comes natural. They can't help it. Hormones build up inside them. Testosterone. It does that. Anyway, a man's supposed to rule the roost and do whatever he wants. Everyone knows that. Boys were raised that way, right from the start. Women know they've made their beds, so no use complaining about lying inside them. It's been like that forever. Women always knew what the world was like and shouldn't complain.

"When you were little I had a job where I could keep you in a carriage beside me, but when you got bigger I tried one daycare after another trying to find one I could afford, and workers to take good care of you. That was most important, because you're my most precious possession. Waitresses don't make much money, so I needed someone to help pay the bills.

"We got lucky finding Mort. A roof over our heads, food in the fridge, clothes on our backs. Lots of people don't have that. Anyway Amanda, hush up. If he hadn't hit me, he might have hit you. Ever think about that?"

"Yeah, Momma. I think about it a lot."

Mort used to twang on a beat-up guitar. Kept singing some old song with a *slap her down again* chorus, and all his buddies laughed and sang along. Sorry, Mort. Those days are gone now, extinct like dodo birds. After an ice age nicer days always come along.

But Momma still needs a man in her life. I'm not enough. She'd be back with Mort in a minute if there wasn't a restraining order. She keeps making excuses. "It wasn't Mort's fault. His father used to beat him, so he grew up needing to hit back. He had to smack someone. I was all he'd got."

Before Mort came along we were poor, but Momma always seemed kind of carefree, singing along to radio songs, sometimes even dancing. Maybe she was just pretending to be happy, but I want her like that again. Even if she's not really happy, I want her to pretend just for my sake. I'm that selfish.

I want to ask her about my own daddy. What was he like? Was he mean like Mort? And if he was a nice man, how come he didn't stick around?

But she gets upset if I ask about him, so I pretend I don't wonder anything, that I don't think children have fathers. As if I believe babies just appear inside their mother's bellies like magic, like Mary in the Bible.

As if we don't learn sex education in school.

Another subject is ancient history. It turns out that democracy started long ago in Greece where everyone voted and had free speech. But then the teacher remembered exceptions, and mentioned them, casual, like a footnote in a textbook, or a postscript tacked on at the end of a letter. "Except for women, of course," he said. "Except for slaves."

The minute I finish high school I want to move as far away as I can, the way Momma did at my age. I'll be eighteen and all grown up so the police can't make me come home.

That's what I want, but it was different for Momma. Her sister watched out for Gramma. If I went away, who would look after Momma then?

A woman wakes up and opens her eyes. It doesn't help; the world is still black. Is she alive or is she dead? She needs to know this.

She can't move; not an arm, a hand, not even her little finger. Her mind is still capable of giving orders, but her body refuses to obey. Or is unable.

She tries to make a sound. Nothing happens.

So this is what death is like, she thinks. What she has seen happen to her parents as she held their hands and watched them die.

Mort lies beside her, peaceful, unaware of what is happening. He's a light sleeper; if she could make a sound he'd hear her and know something's wrong, dial 9-1-1.

Or she hopes he's beside her, that she's in a bed, not a coffin. She needs to believe that she's in bed.

Again and again she tries to tighten her throat, to make a sound. Then finally a low moan escapes her throat, so quiet she can hardly hear it. And now she relaxes, is able to move, can reach for the bedside lamp. Light appears, like a blessing, a benediction.

Mort stirs, blinks, grumbles, "What the hell's going on?"

"Nothing. Go back to sleep."

"Well, I can't until you turn off that damn light."

This feels like a pivotal moment, an epiphany. Unexpected. Unwanted, even. She thinks of Paul on the Damascus road.

She has been so close to death, and knows life will never be the same again. She will appreciate everything, take nothing for granted. She will change her life, be strong, ask Mort to leave. Of course she will. But by the time morning comes she'll decide it was just a bad dream; an hour later it will have been forgotten.

A woman drives a car into the night. There must be some reason why she does this.

The windows are wide open, and her long hair blows across her eyes like a heavy veil. This could be dangerous, she thinks, but keeps on driving, anyway. She tries to imagine what she looks like: a witch, maybe, or someone with a wig worn backwards. If there was anyone to see. If there were any oncoming headlights.

Sometimes she takes one hand from the wheel and runs her fingers through her hair like a comb. "That's better," she says to no one.

She could fasten her hair into a ponytail with an elastic band. Other drivers would be safer, and pedestrians, and small animals that roam the world at night. Roadkill: it would be so easy to prevent it.

Perhaps an elastic band is in her purse. She checks the seat beside her but can't find her purse. She gropes around on the floor in case it has fallen down. When she turns to check the back seat the car swerves like a warning.

Maybe they had a fight. Perhaps supper was cold or overcooked. Lately this often happens. She gets distracted. Her mind slips into neutral: food burns, the kettle boils dry.

She checks her arms for sore spots, feels her cheekbones and around her eyes. Bruises come later, after the pain has gone. Always they surprise her. Her skin is white and then it's not. Bruises rise toward the surface of her skin, like stones emerging from beneath a field. She stayed at someone's farm when she was a child and remembers the stillness of those empty fields, and being surrounded by so much space. The sweet innocence of childhood.

Her feet are cold. She isn't wearing shoes. Where are they?

Once she was a child and memorized a poem about some boy with bare feet. He probably had freckles on his face and carried a fishing pole over his shoulder like Tom Sawyer or Huckleberry Finn. Once she was a child and envied boys who could walk barefoot and go fishing, but she got used to it. There's nothing she can't get used to, because she's strong.

She says this aloud so she will really and truly believe it, and tries to recognize her voice.

What in the world is she doing? Where is she? She is driving a car. Whose car? Somebody must own it. A man, of course. Where is he?

Tom Sawyer could make his friends whitewash a fence. Men have this power; they can make you do anything.

Darkness is everywhere: inside her mind, outside the car. She keeps driving.

She shivers, and wishes she had a coat. She closes the window beside her, but the one on the passenger side is wide open. It'll be hard to turn the handle while she's driving, but she tries anyway. The car swerves toward the ditch and then swerves back.

She is still shivering, and wonders how to work the heater; she slides levers one way and another while the car swerves back and forth. Swerve right; correct for this. Swerve left; correct for that.

Finally heat surrounds her but it doesn't help. The warmth touches her skin, but doesn't reach inside her body to thaw her frozen bones. She needs coffee. To drink, of course, but mainly to move the paper container back and forth from one cold hand to the other.

Oh no! She notices she's only wearing a nylon nightie. No wonder she's so cold. Now she can't go into a restaurant to warm up. Not in a nightgown. But she's so cold she might risk it, if a coffee shop was open, if she was on a busy city street

where she might find one, instead of lost in this empty coun-
tryside on a dark road that seems to go nowhere.

She feels beside her. No cell phone. It must be inside her
missing purse.

She'd better find a pay phone and call to reassure him that
she's okay. He must be worried. She practises aloud the words
she will say. "Hiya. It's me. I'm all right." Perhaps he has
not even noticed her disappearance. After all, it seems to be
the middle of the night. The phone will ring on and on, until
finally he wakes up and stumbles toward the phone, groggy
with sleep. "Who is this?" he'll ask, and then she'll say her
name, whatever it is. Right this minute she can't remember.
She's cold and shivering. That must be why.

"Don't be silly," she could say, stalling for time. "It's me."

Maybe then he'll say her name. Some word that starts with
L, she thinks. He might say, "Hi Lorraine. Where are you?"
Or perhaps Lois or Louise. "Oh, Laura, I've been so worried."
"Lee Anne! Thank god you're safe." Or else he won't. "Who
is this?" he'll ask again, and she'll say, "Guess. Who do you
think?" and finally he will tell her.

She wants to phone him and find out, but has no coins for
a pay phone. Anyway, she can't remember the number to call.

Or she could phone her daughter. Doesn't she have a daughter? She isn't sure.

She continues driving. She checks the fuel gauge; there is lots
of gasoline. "Always look on the bright side," someone once
told her, her mother maybe, when she was a child, whenever
that was.

She tries to look on the bright side now: she has a car, gasoline, knows how to drive.

Bruise-woman is in a shelter again. Perhaps this time she won't
return to whatever guy keeps battering her.

A nice policewoman brought her in and advised her to stay
put. The folks who run the shelter try to convince her to stay

for a while, at least until the bruises fade a little, but no one is betting on that.

They offer alternatives. She could hide out with her sister where she would be safe. Perhaps a relative could drive some sense into her head.

But Bruise-woman keeps apologizing for him, saying it was her fault. The counsellors are not surprised: battered women always do this. But this time it was probably true. Mort found an unmailed letter and didn't like what she'd written about him and said he'd give her something to write about.

He's probably still living in the apartment, but what about Amanda, her sweet teenage daughter? Is she with him? Or is she safe, bunking with a classmate? If so, which one? No one seems to know. Bruise-woman is frantic, and decides to go home and try to find her.

Probably she would have gone back anyway.

Cathay

JOSEPHINE FINDS A LIBRARY BOOK about Marco Polo and suddenly, even though she is only fourteen years old, she comes up with a plan for the rest of her life; she will travel to Cathay the way Marco did, and write down all her adventures in a diary. The Great Khan must be dead by now, but probably there are lots of other interesting people to meet. Then, years and years later, when she turns into a sweet, white-haired old lady, too frail for the perils of exploration, she can write about her adventures in a book that will be placed in all the libraries of the world. She will become famous like Marco Polo, and inspire other youngsters to a life of travel and adventure.

Marco called his destination Cathay, but he was wrong about the name. Josephine knows he was really visiting China.

China is strange and exotic. Josephine knows this from pictures in the *National Geographic*. China has an enormous wall. Special birds called Peking ducklings swim in the famous Yangtze river. Women carry umbrellas because of sunshine instead of rain, and the old ones walk with tiny steps because tight bandages had been wrapped around their feet. Chinese children are beautiful; their straight black hair is cut in bangs, just like Josephine's.

Missionaries go there to tell the Chinese people the good news about God and Jesus. When they come back to Canada on holiday, they give talks at church and show pictures on a big screen: rice paddies, pagodas, and sweet little Chinese children with their newly-Christian parents. If Josephine became a missionary she would have to save heathen souls for Jesus, but she doesn't like that idea; it's too bossy. Marco Polo didn't try to change the people he met; he simply wrote down what he saw, the way a newspaper reporter would.

Now, when neighbours ask what she's going to be when she grows up, Josephine will have a magnificent travelling plan to report. "I don't know" had never impressed them. "I don't care" was what she'd meant.

To be a missionary, Josephine will have to speak Chinese and believe, really truly believe, in God and Jesus. She will need to think those Bible stories aren't just fairy tales, but really true. This is a problem, because unfortunately Josephine doesn't quite believe in God. Not in the way she believes in trees and sparrows and squirrels, things she can actually see in her own neighbourhood. At Sunday School, she sings along with all the others: "God sees the little sparrow fall," even though she doesn't believe it. Surely God must have more important things to do, like watching out for wars and making sure the good guys always win. Anyway, why just sparrows? What about all the other birds? And squirrels, June bugs, earthworms? What about people? And what if several creatures fell down at the same time? How could God watch them all? Surely this would happen; there are so many birds and animals and insects just in Canada, and lots more in the rest of the world.

Sunday School teachers sing those words too, and seem to believe them. But maybe not. They might be just pretending, but not want to admit it.

Nanny and Gramps go to Baptist church and sing hymns that are different from the ones at United. Baptist people are saved upstairs inside that church, their bodies dunked under water in a bathtub. The curtain is closed, but everyone stares at the window where it is happening.

Nanny's dear sweet daughter died of diphtheria when she was little. Nanny says she's up in heaven, waiting for Nanny and Gramps to come and join her. That death happened years ago, but apparently the little girl is still two years old and patiently waiting. Josephine feels sorry for that poor little kid, with no momma to cuddle her and rock her to sleep, no papa to bounce her on his knee, no brothers and sisters to play with. But Nanny says she's not lonely because there are lots of other children in heaven. Nanny believes everything the preacher says with her whole heart.

All her relatives are believers, so Josephine doesn't want to tell them that all those Jesus stories seem ridiculous, like the crazy things that happened to Alice when she fell down a rabbit hole, or to Dorothy and Toto in the Land of Oz.

Josephine decides to put off the believing in God part, and start learning the language. After all, how hard can Chinese be? It was so easy to learn English that she can't remember anyone teaching her. Of course there are boring grammar lessons at school, clauses and verbs and prepositions, but that's not the way people really talk.

Josephine knows she is lucky to work in the library after school where she is sure to find the information she needs. She puts books back on the shelves according to the numbers on their spines. Most of her friends don't even know there is a Dewey Decimal System for perfect filing. But it's only for non-fiction; novels are put away in alphabetical order according to the writer's last name. At first, Josephine filed them alphabetically by title, until some old busybody complained.

Josephine can't find any books about teaching yourself Chinese, and eventually asks the youngest librarian, the one who smiles and seems the nicest. But when Josephine asks where to look, the librarian's smile keeps getting bigger until finally she laughs out loud. The head librarian glares at them, and puts her finger against her lips, meaning SILENCE!

There are SILENCE signs on all the library tables, and Josephine knows they are both in trouble.

She never mentions the subject again, but keeps her eyes

open and discovers autobiography. It turns out that some other people have visited Cathay and written books about it. Sometimes they list Chinese words at the back of the book. Whenever Josephine finds a book like this she signs it out and copies those words into a notebook.

This has to be a secret. Momma must never suspect because she worries whenever Josephine is out of her sight. When Josephine sets off on a bike ride she has to tell exactly where she's going and exactly when she'll return. Her mother certainly wouldn't let her travel all the way to China. Marco went to Cathay with his father and uncle, but Papa would never quit work to take such a long trip. His job is too important; it's how he makes the money to pay for food and clothes for the family. And Momma would never leave her nice house and bridge club. She'd probably lock Josephine in a closet if that was the only way to keep her safe at home.

When she climbs in bed each night Josephine thinks about a Chinese word. While she's asleep her brain will keep repeating the word all night long, and by morning will have memorized it perfectly. Josephine has heard of this simple trick in a *Reader's Digest* magazine and is sure that it will work.

At first she also records the Chinese alphabet symbols, but these are too difficult and slow her down. Anyway she only wants to speak the language, not read it. Maybe there are complicated grammar and spelling rules, but Marco wouldn't have known them either.

Sometimes Josephine gets discouraged. It takes such a long time to learn the language at one word a day, three hundred and sixty-five a year. However, in only four years she will be eighteen years old, finally a grown-up, and no one will be able to stop her from leaving home. By then she will know more than a thousand words. Then she will write down Chinese conversations and create an up-to-date book that will be really useful.

Around this time she begins reading newspapers and discovers that some missionaries are being killed. Killed! The Bible tells about killings that happened hundreds of years ago, and the Catholic kids at school tell terrible stories of how holy martyrs were burned at the stake or boiled in oil. Those tortures happened just because they loved God. Does she really love him that much? Of course not. She's not even sure God is real. How can people expect her to believe in someone she can't see?

Anyway, Chinese people have their own religion; they believe in Buddha or Confucius, instead of God or Jesus. If Josephine had been born in China she would believe in their religion, too, and wouldn't like people trying to make her change it. She'd get pretty mad. Of course she wouldn't kill them. She'd just yell at them to go home and leave her alone.

So Josephine rips up her pages of Chinese words and decides to learn French instead. At the library she has heard of Gertrude Stein and Ernest Hemingway. Maybe they still live in Paris and she could drop in for a visit. She could interview them and take snapshots, and maybe become a journalist or a famous photographer with pictures in *Life Magazine*. Momma sings about the last time she saw Paris, even though she's never been there, so if she doesn't want her daughter to go so far away Josephine could always take her along.

Paris is probably closer than China.

Dawn

DAWN'S HAIR IS AS YELLOW as a canary and she sings whenever she wants to, like right now on the Dufferin bus: "*Where have all the flowers gone?*" She looks around her and it's really true. No flowers here. No blossoms tossing toward the grimy windows of the bus searching for sunshine, no vine tendrils stretching up to the ceiling.

Dawn's hair is as yellow as a magic marker, bright as food dye. She is sitting still, travelling nowhere, trying not to care where Charley is.

Roly can't help but pay attention. He noticed her the minute he got on and has been staring down at her ever since. There are empty seats, but he stands beside her seat anyway. Her hair is so short, the shortest hair he's ever seen. Maybe an inch long at the most. He is almost mesmerized by its strangeness. He reaches his hand down to almost touch it. She is singing a sad refrain: "*When will they ever learn? When will they ever learn?*" ignoring him and everyone else.

Dawn's hair is ragged because she cut it last night after drinking too much beer. Dawn is tiny, five foot nothing, and seldom drinks beer, so probably one bottle should have been her max.

She drank the first one to relax, so she wouldn't yell at Charley when he finally ambled home. Time went by and she got angry all over again. She drank a second beer to calm down, and so on. At four in the morning she decided to cut her hair. Why not? Why the heck not?

Charley always said he loved her long blonde hair. So there! So there! One sip of beer, one chop of the scissors. Sip, chop. Sip, chop. Cutting by feel. She couldn't see because of all the tears sloshing out of her eyes and down her face. Sometimes chopping off only a little bit, sometimes almost to the scalp.

Cutting with dull rusty scissors. Muttering, "Damn stupid scissors," under her breath. Meaning, damn stupid Charley.

In the morning, she rolled over and discovered still no Charley in bed beside her, nests of hair in the bed instead, rusted scissors on the floor beside her slippers, the shorn head of a stranger in the bathroom mirror.

"*Where have all the flowers gone?*" Dawn sings that first verse over and over because she has somehow forgotten the rest of the song. Where have all the other words gone? Also her hair? How long will it take before it reaches her shoulders again? She remembers her ponytail, and sheds one tear and then another before she forces herself to stop.

Now she is riding a bus going nowhere, wherever the bus driver decides. She should go back. Charley will be angry if she's not there when he gets home.

Roly keeps staring at her hair. He's never seen a hairstyle like it before. Such a bright yellow, like dandelions in summer. And so bright and shiny. He wants to reach out and touch, feel its dandelion softness against his fingers. Probably it would be soft and warm, like touching summer in mid-winter. What jazzy hair. This woman has style; she has pizzazz. She knows who she is and what she wants to look like; she is special. He's got to get to know her.

Phlegm begins to rattle in his throat and he needs to cough it up again. He tries to clear his throat quietly, politely, so little dandelion princess won't be offended by the sound. Damn Greek cigarettes, he thinks, I gotta switch to something mild.

What if he skipped work today? This dandelion princess is more important. He has never missed a day, not once in fifteen years, never phoned in sick. He has never even been late. But why the hell not? Let them get along without him for a change. Suddenly everybody will realize how hard he always works. Let's see them try to manage without him, fill all the requisitions without making mistakes, ship out all the orders themselves.

He could get off at the same stop as she does, watch which office she goes into, and then just happen to be standing outside when she gets off work. Spend all day long sitting in a coffee shop across the street, watching for her out the window, and trying to figure out how to strike up a conversation.

Maybe: "Mind telling me where you get your hair done? My sister's always wanted a style like that." Dandelion princess will politely tell him her hairdresser. And then what? Then what?

Or: "I don't have a paper to write that hairdresser name down. Can we go into that coffee shop across the street so I can write it on a paper napkin?" So they go into a coffee shop, he writes the name down, and then what?

Of course he buys her a cup of coffee. Tells her, "It's the least I can do. My sister will be so happy to get that hairdresser name."

Maybe dandelion princess asks his sister's name. He'd better think up a name to tell her. Maybe he could make up a whole story about his fake sister: how she had one miscarriage after another, and has a husband who hits her, but only on the back so the bruises won't show. A jazzy hairstyle would perk her right up. Maybe she'd get to believe she was important. Maybe she'd leave that no-good bum.

Dawn feels in her pocket. Oh no! She forgot her wallet. She pulls out her plastic token holder and can't believe it's empty. How is she going to get home?

Maybe she could stay on this bus until the end of the line, then pretend she'd been asleep and missed her stop, so could she please just stay right here on this bus while it travels back to the station again?

She tries to see what the bus driver looks like. Old and grumpy? Young and mean? But she can't look because a man is standing close beside her holding onto the pole behind her with one hand and the pole in front with the other. He's blocking her in so tight she feels a little claustrophobic and wants to rush past him out the door to grab some freedom. But no, she can't get off the bus. Not without any money or tokens. She'd better stay put. He can stand there if he wants to.

Roly stares down at the dandelion hair and imagines what happens when this little princess turns old. Will her hair turn puffy and white like dandelion fluff. Then he remembers how dandelion fluff blows away and quickly switches to another image: a green hillside somewhere, dotted with dandelion flowers or buttercups. Him and the dandelion princess all alone on that grassy hillside, touching each other all over, making love. Afterward he'll be so excited that he'll tumble down that hill like a little kid, rolling over and over. At the bottom he'll be so dizzy he can hardly stand up. Dandelion princess watches him and laughs, then tries it herself. They climb back up the hill together, rest awhile, and then make love again.

A voice calls, "Better get off, folks. End of the line."

"Oh no," Dawn says, faking amazement. "I wasn't paying attention and missed my stop. Can I just stay on the bus and ride back?"

Roly is startled. Things are happening way too fast. "Me too," he says.

"Sorry folks. This is my last run of the morning. This bus is going out of service. Wait across the street and catch the next one going back. You've just missed one. Another will be along in half an hour."

"At least give us some transfers," Dawn says.

Us. Roly glances around. There are only two passengers on this bus: dandelion princess and himself. Roly grins. Dandelion princess said, "Give *us* some transfers," just as though they're travelling together. It's a good sign.

The bus driver hands them transfers and they get off.

Half an hour until the next bus. Roly looks around. There's

a coffee shop on the corner. It'll have paper serviettes where he can write down the hairdresser name.

Dandelion princess interrupts his thoughts. "I forgot my wallet. Could you buy me a coffee? I'll pay you back later."

Dawn's hair is bright yellow, nearly as blinding as the sun. As they head toward the coffee shop, Roly reaches out and almost touches it. He can hardly believe his luck.

Dome Car

SOMEWHERE THERE IS AN OLD BOYFRIEND Val can hardly remember. Perhaps he still exists, miles and time zones behind her. If she concentrated really hard she might remember his face, his name. But not right now; not while sitting in the back seat of the dome car with a guy she met two days ago.

So casual; his arm resting easily behind her, touching, then not quite touching, her shoulder, then touching it again. This takes place whenever the train lurches, while Val acts nonchalant, trying to behave the same as all the other tourists in the dome car, gawking at the huge snow-topped mountains that surround them. She pretends nothing is happening, and thinks, probably nothing is.

Only a couple of days. But their life seems so intimate. Val is always aware of him. In the coach, in the seat across from her, restless, stretching, thrashing about, trying to get comfortable, finally heading to the bathroom, returning, coughing, wandering off to the smoking area. She can smell tobacco smoke when he returns.

There are no pillows; they are only provided to first-class passengers. Economy-class travellers don't have blankets either, although the ticket agent had assured her that they would receive them. The passengers struggle all night long. They flail this way and that, folding their coats under their heads, then getting cold, retrieving them again to use as blankets. They tip the seat back farther, try the footrest up high for a while, then down again. There's a loud thump whenever this happens. A woman drops a bottle of pills, then flounders about on the floor trying to find them, giggling to cover her embarrassment. By morning everyone is exhausted.

But anyway, what does it matter? Val is travelling across Canada, westward, chasing the sunset, crossing time zones. Each day changing her watch backward another hour, extending the trip. Who knows what time it really is? Or which day? It seems this train ride might go on forever, and now Val wishes it would.

She hardly spoke to him the first day, but now chatters nonstop. She has spent more hours next to this man than she has ever spent with her old boyfriend, that man she can hardly remember. More time than with her friends or the folks at work. She can hardly remember them, either.

She is travelling through time and space, through the landscape of the country and of her mind. Scenery opens and engulfs her, then disappears behind the train, already forgotten as she absorbs, is absorbed by, a new vista.

She is lusting for this stranger, now, as they leave Jasper, the dome car crowded, everyone staring at one peak or another, pointing them out. The oohs and aahs, people swivelling around, staring at something which may or may not be Mount Rundle, the highest mountain in some place or other, Alberta maybe, or North America. Wherever. Are they still in Alberta? Or maybe British Columbia already. As if it matters. The engineer will get them to the west coast, has probably travelled this route hundreds of times. She wishes he'd slow the train down because she's not in a hurry to get there, wherever *there* is; the end of the line. She wants this trip, this moment, to continue on and on forever; the man's arm along the back of her seat, and now descending a little, curving around her shoulder, as she leans into him slightly, so casually, it could almost be accidental, due to the motion of the train. Her head rests lightly against

CAROL MALYON

his shoulder, because she is so tired from all those sleepless
nights in the coach, aware of him tossing and turning, while
she tosses and turns, too, wanting to hold him, to be held, as
they lull each other to sleep....

And now his arm really is around her, and his hand, oh surely
not, is slightly cupping her breast, and everyone is turning in
their direction in order to gaze at some snow-topped mountain
or other, while she pretends nothing is happening, acting cool
and casual until all those heads swivel forward again, and now
his finger is stroking her nipple, circling around and around,
feeling it stiffen, and it is hard for her to sit still; she feels so
restless all of a sudden, and knows she ought to move to a
different seat, but the dome car is too crowded, and anyway
she doesn't want to. Home is so very far away, and this guy
so very close.

Travelling beside mountains that were thrust upward a million
years ago. "This was once an ocean floor," he murmurs. "Can you
believe it?" And she can; she can believe anything he tells her.

Mountains and landscapes and old memories are gradually
eroding. She and this man are travelling together, moving
backward through time zones, flowing back into prehistory,
toward the dawn of time, where nothing else seems to matter,
especially the goddamn tourists in the seats up front who keep
swivelling their heads around, not wanting to miss a single
mountain top, as if they don't all look the same by now; seen
one, seen them all. The passengers chattering anyway, exclaim-
ing, "Ooh, just look at that," and now she begins murmuring
too. "Ooh," she says, "Oh yes, oh yes."

She thinks of fairy tales, the way they always begin: Once
upon a time.... This is the prince she has been waiting for.
Their names begin with the same letter; it seems a good omen,
as though they were meant to find each other, to be together.
But fairy tales leave out so many details, like whether or not
the prince is married.

They arrive in Vancouver. He disappears.

The Keel Hides Underneath
the Water with the Fish

THE SAILBOAT IS WHERE Sandra chooses to begin.
Once upon a time there was a man, there was a woman. They went sailing. A storm came out of nowhere, so it took them longer to get to shore than they had expected. The woman had a date with someone else that evening. She was late. Perhaps this was the beginning of the end of that relationship. Later she married the man who had taken her sailing.

Sandra's mother and father are dead now and Sandra is the only proof that they existed. This is the task of children, she thinks. While they live they bear witness; they provide proof. Sandra is childless. When she dies she will erase their existence, as well as her own.

Once upon a time a man invited a woman to go sailing. He knew what he was doing. She had to be home by a certain time, but he pretended to have trouble getting back to shore. She was late for her date. Finally she married the man with the sailboat. Later he was unhappy but had only himself to blame.

Sandra's parents are dead, and the ancestors who begat them. Sandra imagines a family Bible with a long listing of begats. It ends with Sandra who has control. She can change their stories to her own purpose. Everyone does this.

Once upon a time a woman went sailing with another man to make her boyfriend jealous. Perhaps she was trying to prod her boyfriend into proposing or breaking up. Perhaps she liked both men, or only one of them, or neither. Or perhaps she simply wanted to go sailing, and accepted whoever asked her first. These things may be true, or they may not be: a woman wanted to miss her date, a man wanted her to miss it.

Sandra owns her parents now, and owns their stories. She can tell them in ways that favour her father or her mother, or favour neither. No one will contradict her. Perhaps Sandra will be kind to them, and make them beautiful and innocent, young dreamers drifting toward love.

But Sandra has memories that are difficult to erase.

When Grandma comes to visit, she and Sandra's mother look at albums of faded photographs. The women sit at the kitchen table all afternoon. They pour tea from a chipped enamel teapot, and they talk about the old days when Sandra's mother attracted all the boys like bees to honey and Grandma invited the boyfriends to stay for supper.

"Remember Billy Gladstone?" says Sandra's mother.

"Was he the one who played rugby?" Grandma asks. "The one with a sister named Shirley who married one of the Baker boys on Beech Street? I think the other Baker boy worked at the bank."

When Grandma has fastened Billy Gladstone in her memory, when she knows which street he lived on and where he went to church, when she remembers that he's the nephew of Mrs. Watson in her chapter of Eastern Star, then the story can get started.

All these stories start out the same. Men fall in love with Sandra's mother who sits on a wicker rocking chair and ignores them. She wears a straight dress with ruffles along the hem. Her hair is bobbed, and shaped in perfect Marcel waves. Men flock around her; they hang around her house hoping to be invited to stay for supper.

All the stories have the same ending. Sandra's mother smokes a cigarette and stares out the kitchen window and wonders what life would be like if she had married Billy Gladstone or Joey Wilson or Chuck McDonald.

"But I wouldn't be here," Sandra reminds her. These are either the first words she has spoken, or else the first words her mother and grandmother have noticed.

Her mother looks at Sandra strangely, as though she wonders who Sandra is, then finally remembers. "Of course you'd be here. You'd just have a different dad."

Sandra knows this isn't true. She looks like her father and has his temper. Everyone says so. She would be different inside and out if she had a different father.

"I don't want a different dad," she says.

Then Sandra's mother gets fed up and tells her to stop being so silly; they were just talking and having a bit of fun. And anyway, can't she have a conversation with her own mother without Sandra butting in.

"In my day," says Grandma, "children were seen and not heard." Grandma always talks this way: "Little pitchers have big ears." "Spare the rod and spoil the child."

"For one thing," says Grandma, "I'd do something about the way she walks. Stand up straight," she tells Sandra. "Don't slouch. Pull back those shoulders."

Sometimes Grandma marches in a parade with other ladies from Eastern Star. She looks straight ahead and pretends she can't see Sandra watching from the sidewalk. Sandra stares at those Eastern Stars. They wear white dresses, and are old and fat and ugly. After they pass by Sandra falls in behind them and imitates the way they march. She follows them all the way to the park by Ashton Bay where they disband. She watches the Eastern Stars pull out their white lace handkerchiefs and wipe the sweat off their red faces.

Those Eastern Stars are dead now, and Ashton Bay has disappeared. Another bay with the same name has replaced it. The new bay doesn't stink because a sewage plant has been built beside it. Sailboats are moored in a marina in neat rows. The wooden walkways seem brand-new, as though they are replaced every year instead of growing old.

Sandra walks on an old wharf in her childhood. It is made of huge squared timbers that are greenish-black and slippery. The black colour could be from age or weather or from the same preservative that's used on telephone poles and railway ties. Water is choppy, and slops over the dock. Green algae grows inside crevices and all along the edges of every piece of wood. The catwalk boards are rotten. Pieces are missing, and the boards feel spongy beneath Sandra's feet. This is part of the adventure for Sandra who goes sailing with her father every chance she gets.

Each fall the sailboats are brought ashore and propped up on tall racks for the winter. The decks are high above Sandra's head, and tall keels curve beneath them like fins of giant fish.

When Sandra sees sailboats on the lake she thinks about the keels hidden beneath the water. Some of the children in the schoolyard don't believe in their existence. They think the part they see above the water is all there is. For once Sandra knows an extra piece of truth. From the corner of the schoolyard she studies the different shadings of the lake.

Sandra plays in her bedroom so she won't mess up the house that's clean for bridge club. She makes up stories about her paper dolls; the Shirley Temple doll is named Sandra.

Once upon a time a man and a woman fell in love. They knew they would be perfect for each other and so they married. They thought that they were happy and didn't know something was missing. But then they had a baby and life was perfect. The family kept pictures in an album. The couple with their arms around each other's waist. The woman cradling the baby in her arms. The man holding the baby on his knee. All three of them together. You can see smiles on all their faces and know how happy they always were.

This is the story. It starts out once upon a time. Other details could be included. The family lived in a white frame house. A maple tree shaded the back garden. Petunias bloomed in flower boxes beneath each window. In winter they sat by the fireplace; they made popcorn and drank hot chocolate. They played checkers and listened to music.

Sandra tells this story to people that she meets. This is the way mythology was passed on among the ancients, before there was a way to write things down.

Leaves

MAGGIE IS THINKING ABOUT MICHAEL, and also J. Alfred Prufrock.[1] J. Alfred is not a real person of course, and Maggie is the one resembling Prufrock, indecisive, wavering. Michael is not like Prufrock at all. But there it is: Maggie is thinking of both him and Michael, but mainly of Michael. She is remembering how they met.

They met so often; they didn't meet often enough. Each encounter seemed unique, memorable, each meeting a new beginning.

They met on a subway platform waiting for an eastbound train. "Why eastbound?" he asked her, and she asked him the same thing. They got off at the same subway stop. Sometimes she thinks this is how it all began.

Or they met on a streetcar, each heading for the same empty seat. He reached it first, so she sat down on his lap.

They actually met in a neighbourhood coffee shop.

Later she ran into him everywhere: at the local cinema, in one bookstore and then another. Maggie keeps wondering which meeting was the most important and changed her life, but anyway, what difference does it make?

"We can't go on meeting like this," she told him, but she was wrong.

They met at art galleries and museums and cinemas and in bed. That was the best part. They planned casual encounters and assumed they fooled everyone. They fooled no one.

They ran into each other often and everywhere; then he got sick and they didn't.

"I've been looking for you everywhere," Maggie intended to tell him the next time they met, if she ever found him again. And if we could meet, Maggie wondered, would we have anything in common except our sordid little affair? Would it begin all over again? Of course not, she thought, but she was lying and she knew it.

If only.... If only he hadn't had a wife, a child, another life. If only this, if only that. If only he hadn't gotten sick.

If Maggie met J. Alfred Prufrock they could compare their pathetic coffee-spoon lives. Maggie could describe her encounters with Michael, their meetings that didn't happen often enough, that never lasted long enough.

She will always wonder, if only: if only they could start all over again, on a train, in a streetcar, wherever, would it be possible to change the ending? Would she admit how much she needed him? Could she have dared to eat that peach?

But so what? It doesn't matter. Michael is gone now, gone forever, and it's too late.

Maggie is thinking of love. Well, not really. She is thinking of lust. She is thinking of how much she wants Michael, now, right this minute. But always, in the back of her mind, she knows that if he were here, if they had each other, and relaxed, let themselves drift, if they dissolved into each other's bodies again, blissed out, their voices blending in a sweet glossolalia of confusion, it would soon, too soon, be over. And then what? He would leave.

He'd be here and then he'd be gone. Because Michael has another life. Maggie had known this from the beginning, but somehow that doesn't make it easier to let him go. She keeps thinking about this. She is thinking too much. Right now imagining is the best part, the only part.

She is remembering them together, imagining they are still

together. They simply follow their instincts and everything is so much better than it has ever been before. She doesn't have to say, "Gentle. I need it gentle," or, "Oh yes, keep doing what you're doing. Don't ever stop." She doesn't need to because he knows, and they are travelling together, floating through endless time and empty space, soaring close, too close (be careful!) to the sun. Their bodies attuned, keyed together, like precious antique violins: Amati, Stradivari.... They are as innocent as little children, holding hands, skipping, dancing.... And laughing; they can't stop laughing at everything, at themselves and the world, such a sweet ridiculous place.

But this is not what is happening, not at all.

Because already it is tomorrow and Maggie's lover has disappeared. He was supposed to meet her hours ago. He's not at work. His cell phone rings on and on unanswered. Where could he be? This isn't like him.

Perhaps he is ill, fastened by tubes to a hospital bed, gasping, unable to communicate. Perhaps he has drifted into a coma, an empty dream. "Blink your eyes if you understand," someone could be saying, but either he can't blink or can't understand. Or both. His wife and children would be at his bedside, the wife weeping, praying, holding his hand.

Or perhaps his mind isn't empty at all, but has simply travelled away, slipped into some other world where Maggie no longer exists. He has forgotten her completely, left her far, too far, behind. Maggie knows people can emerge from comas and be fine, just as before; nothing changed. But sometimes they are never the same again.

Perhaps he is already dead. Oh, my god, no. Please not that. Not the finality of the coffin and cremation. Not the eulogies. The weeping reminiscences shared by the wife and family, the acceptable friends.

On the CD player Van Morrison is singing, "Baby, please don't go," and now Maggie is singing along, inventing as she goes, off-key as always. "*Oh no! Baby, please don't go! Don't leave me behind, between these crisp pristine white sheets, to once again become chaste and virginal as a nun.*" Maybe later, years and years later. But please not right now. Not while she is yearning for one more moon dance.

Tomorrow, should tomorrow ever come, there will be a lunar eclipse, the moon playing hide and seek with the earth's shadow: catch me if you can. If the cloud cover lifts, watchers will be able to see a reddish glow, a warm memory of the moon. Maggie wonders about the ancients; how could they have interpreted such a terrifying heavenly event? The reliable moon, high in the sky as always, but then, (oh no!) gradually swallowed by utter blackness. They plead with medicine men, gurus, witch doctors, anyone: beg them to do something, anything, sacrifice a lamb, a maiden; whatever it takes to bring the moon back. Hurry! Let's pray! Fall on our knees, quick, before it's too late. Repent, damn it, repent. Scream at the heavens. Weep. Promise the moon anything at all if it will please return again.

Maggie feels like a sacrificed maiden herself.

And miracle of miracles! Apparently those desperate prayers were able to propitiate the gods. Oh, thank you! Blessings upon you, whoever, whatever you are. And welcome back, sweet moon, as once again it travels its same old path across the sky.

Tomorrow, if all goes well, an eclipse will happen, according to some universal plan. Traditionally, this is a time to make a wish. And Maggie does, and she prays. She actually prays aloud.

She does this, even though Maggie can't understand how people believe in gods or prayers or anything. They do, though: they believe in an absolute mystery. To Maggie, their belief is also a mystery. How dutifully they upend their teacups to read the leafy messages left behind. Maggie believes in the efficiency of tea bags instead.

People consult astrology columns in the newspaper, faithfully, every day; they listen to tarot card messages without laughing aloud. A few friends believe they are psychic, and have admitted this to Maggie, of all people; Maggie, professed atheist, perpetual skeptic.

If they knew about her secret lover they would upend Maggie's teacup or consult a deck of tarot cards to find out what has happened to him. Or study her palm, searching for a broken love line.

But Maggie trusts only science: a cardiologist with a stethoscope would discover her heart was broken.

Maggie is having relationship problems again. *A relationship problem.* Actually, the lack of a relationship. A lack of sex, to be more specific.

"Have you ever noticed," she asks a friend at work, "that people always say they're coming out of a bad relationship? It has become such a cliché. They never say they are coming out of a good one. But it must have been good once. Otherwise why would they have been in it?"

"Well, yeah, but they have to say that. Otherwise you wouldn't give the right response, those small encouraging sounds: *Mmmm hmmm, yeah, uh huh.*"

"And that's another thing. Why do we act sadly sympathetic? Why aren't we happy for them? Why don't we smile and congratulate them? Say 'Wow, that's really terrific. The relationship was bad, and now you're coming out of it? Great! I'm happy for you.'"

"Are you okay?"

"Me? Yeah. I'm great. Except I need another coffee. Be right back." Buying time. Needing to change the subject, to think up some impersonal topic of conversation.

Maggie walks slowly, bent into the wind. Far above her head it is roaring in the branches of the oaks. Sometimes it changes direction and pushes so hard against her that she grabs a tree and hangs on. And the reverberation in her ears; why won't it stop? Maggie arrives home exhausted and out of breath.

All night long she hears the wind roaring in the trees outside her window.

While inside, Maggie is havering.

She discovered the word in a book review that criticized the translator's use of obscure words. Specifically: havering. So Maggie checked the dictionary and discovered it described her. Wavering, hovering. Haver: to vacillate, hesitate.

Hesitating. The way she lives her life.

Maggie knows she's been slightly crazy since Michael disappeared, and looking for someone, anyone, to distract her. She has been using men. Did they notice? Or even care? Would a man consider being used a wish-fulfilment? A woman wanting to have her way with him, meaning sex.

That old cliché: men offer love in order to get sex; women offer sex, but really want love. Both are willing to settle for only one. But their priorities are different.

Men have said that artists draw with their cocks, as if artists are always male. So what do female artists draw with? Pencils, paintbrushes, crayons.... Freud would have said these were simply phallic symbols, artificial cocks. If Freud ever considered that women could be artists. Probably not.

Instead, women were seen as receptacles, containers: of guilt, of semen. Useful, of course, but incapable of action. Subjugated, as in bondage. Sub, as in second-rate, inferior.

Anyway, Maggie is emerging from all that confusion. She's getting stronger. She says, "I'm trying to discover who I really am. I'm finally moving on." Her friends don't bother to ask, "Where to?" They realize she has no idea.

She should have been used to it; they parted so often. It seemed they were always parting, each hello already foreshadowing another goodbye, the bitter aftertaste to each welcoming kiss.

Maggie hadn't seen her sisters for a couple of years, but she'd been desperate, couldn't stand to be alone. She had wept, begged them to come, and finally they agreed.

Two mourning doves were calling to each other, a soft throb beyond the window.

Cottage country, beneath a pale October sky. The wind rising. Leaves struggling against branches, like a flight of birds, panicked, frantic, trying to fly away. The fluttering went on and on; it wouldn't stop.

That desperation. The ominous ring of the phone that morning after Maggie had finally fallen asleep. She was jolted awake, but refused to get up. One of her sisters would have to answer it and take a message. Maggie wasn't brave enough to hear what had happened.

It didn't matter whether she was brave enough or not. Death happens; it happens anyway.

Her sisters told her.

Perhaps Maggie wept or screamed or simply nodded her head. She had known it was bound to happen. It was amazing they'd been able to avoid punishment for so long.

We live in sin; we die in sin. She'd always known they would have to pay. She shivered; ghosts were passing over her grave too.

She tried to think of other things: light, *(love)*, colour, *(love)*, endless space, the moon, the stars, *(love, love, love)*.

The wind blew harder and trees fought against it, their roots fastened deep into the earth, while Maggie watched from a window, and tried to understand how they held on. It should be instinctive, she thought; survival of the fittest. But no one is ever fit enough. Darwin himself dead for a century, maybe more.

She tried to think of beauty *(love)*, of fucking, *(love)*, bodies pressed together against the night. No. Not fucking. She was not going to think about that.

Nevermore. She said it again and again. Nevermore, remembering Poe's raven.[2]

The long fine needles of the northern pines. The waves and shore, and the struggle between them. Water is lovely, dark, and deep. Who wrote that? Or was it the woods? And maybe lonely, dark, and bleak. Dark, anyway. She knows that much.

Water or woods, what difference does it make? Both are dark and deep and unfeeling. Miles to go before she sleeps.[3] Misquoting some poet or other. Frost, probably. It isn't fair; it isn't fair; it isn't fair. Of course not. Why should anything be fair? That ringing phone: someone calling to inform her. She wonders who it had been. Intensive care nurse? Lawyer's secretary? (*In case of death please notify....*) His wife, tight-lipped, released from the bedside?

Because Michael had told no one. Never. Not once. And Maggie had only told her sisters. She'd known they wouldn't approve, of course not, but needed to confide in someone.

He had always worried about getting worse and needing anaesthesia: gradually returning from that unnatural sleep, his wife and family at the bedside, what if he called out her name?

Maggie had tried to reassure him. "It wouldn't matter. You could babble anything, then wake up later and deny it. Blame the anaesthetic, a drug reaction, hallucination, a bad trip."

Maggie can still feel his fingerprints all over her body, semen cooling on her thighs. Hallucinations: she is having them, too.

"Probably I won't survive anyway," he had said. "The chances aren't very good." Then he'd laughed, and expected her to laugh, too.

She kept remembering his smile. His face, his hands, his cock.

The phone rang again. Someone answered it in whispers. Maggie felt like an invalid in a sickroom; in the hall the sisters come and go, not speaking of Michael.[1] Eliot again. They will never mention him again.

Prufrock. Now she can relate to his bleakness and pathetic indecision. All those empty years stretching ahead of her. How will she fill them? Whatever will she do?

She thinks of the stories he tells her in bed. Told her. Past tense, past tense, past tense.

Love is lonely, dark, and bleak.

Early that morning, Maggie had heard knocking at the door and waited for someone to answer it, but nobody did.

Finally she dragged herself out of bed and opened the door. No one was there. Then she noticed a crested bird on a dead pine tree and laughed out loud. "I answered the door to a woodpecker," she told her sisters later. She had laughed and they had, too.

A last laugh. She knew she would never laugh again. *I'll never smile again*, she thought, remembering that sad schmaltzy love song.

Perhaps the rapping happened at the moment Michael died, like in a seance. And what if it did, what if it did?

What about omens and superstitions, gods and spirits? As if it could possibly matter whether she believed in them or not. As if faith could change anything. Things happened. They simply happened. Like the flutter of leaves beyond the window, like waves clutching at the shore of the lake. The earth shuddered a little, but kept on turning.

She shivered, put on a sweater. Someone handed her a cup of tea and urged her to drink it, as if the tea would make a difference.

But nothing will make a difference. Nothing will ever matter. Nevermore. Never again.

And now, the chant:

If there is someone I could have trusted
　　you are the one I would have trusted.

If there was someone who could have saved me
　　you are the one who would have saved me.

A hypnotic rhythm. One breath after another. Each line representing the space of a breath.

If Michael were here speaking these words Maggie would be conscious of his breathing, the length of each sentence, the pause for emphasis, for inhalation. She would be nestled in his arms and murmur "Oh, yes" in the pause after each breath.

If there is someone who....

So many pages. Dozens of them. Hundreds, maybe. Each containing a hand-written couplet.

Incantations. Lamentations. Like verses in an Anglican prayer book: the priest intoning the first line, a pause, then the congregation's response.

If there is someone I could have questioned
  you are the one I would have questioned.

If there is someone who could have answered
  you are the one who would have answered.

Michael hadn't necessarily intended her to have it. His son had forwarded it because her name was on the envelope. But if the words were written to her, about her, surely he wouldn't have left them at home where his family could find them.

Or perhaps he'd explained she was another writer and he wanted her opinion. Probably he had intended to tell Maggie about it: "There's some poetry I've been working on. I've put your name on the cover. If something happens to me, I want you to have it." A conversation that never took place.

The answer may be buried somewhere in these pages, but she cannot bear to read them. Not yet.

Michael Michael Michael....

If there is someone I could have loved
  you are the one I would have loved.

She riffles through the pages. One couplet to a page, hand-written in black ink, in his familiar crisp cursive script.

One couplet per page. So many pages. How many? She has no idea. He hadn't bothered to number them. A sheaf of pages, almost an inch thick: however many pages that is. An inch of incantations. How long could it have taken to write them? Finally she counts them: three hundred and sixty-five. A year's worth, one a day, like vitamins. Perhaps they began on January first, fulfilling a New Year's resolution.

If there is someone who could have shared my pain
　　you are the one who would have shared my pain.

If there is someone who could have healed me
　　you are the one who would have healed me.

She pictures a stage play, a darkened theatre, with a spotlight illuminating one actor and then the other. Each speaks only one couplet, then disappears, swallowed up by blackness.

Two people, a man and a woman. They sit on the stage facing opposite directions, unable to make eye contact. Each couplet could be spoken twice. He speaks the first line, she speaks the second. Then they switch and repeat, with her speaking the first line, and him speaking the second. A repetition as with haiku. Then a pause, the light dims, a moment of darkness before they move on to the next couplet.

The actor sits on the floor, face distorted, hair uncombed, clothes in disarray, pretending to be demented, or possibly not pretending. The actress, also on the floor, unkempt, also pretending or not pretending.

If there is someone who could heal me
　　you are the one who would heal me.

If there is someone I could talk to
　　you are the one I would talk to.

Maggie keeps reading, lost in the rhythm, page after page.

If there is someone who could dream of me.

you are the one who would dream of me.

If there is someone who could weep for me....

And now Maggie is weeping again, her tears falling onto the pages, the ink dissolving. The words blurring into each other and disappearing. As if it matters. As if anything matters. Michael, Michael, Michael. The only person she will ever love.

---

[1]Eliot, T.S. "The Love Song of J. Alfred Prufrock." *Selected Poems* (Penguin Books, nd.).
[2]Edgar Allan Poe, "The Raven." *The Raven and Other Poems* (Scholastic Paperbacks, 2002).
[3]Frost, Robert. "Stopping by Woods on a Snowy Evening." *The Poetry of Robert Frost* (Rinehart and Winston, 1969).

LitCan is Coming

SALLY MEETS A POET. He is five feet tall, her favourite height. He has a beard like all poets; his hair covers his eyes. Sally finds this intriguing. All the men in her life have looked like cocker spaniels; she has never known a sheepdog before.

Sally knows it's her lawyer's fault that she is attracted to this poet. Her lawyer's obsession with details has shown a side of cocker spaniels she doesn't like; he may have ruined them for her forever.

Sally and her poet have a lot in common. They are both unknown. He is waiting for the world to be astonished at his poems; Sally's stories are also waiting.

Her poet lives in Toronto, and Sally suddenly realizes she's always intended to warm up that cold city. It's time to move on, to sell the old family heirloom house in Kingston she has lived in all her life. Old memories and ghosts will be included in the purchase price.

Sally decides her real estate agent must be a woman. Mainly because her lawyer isn't. Spaniel is annoyingly paternal and thinks he's entitled to know everything that happens in her life. Sally wishes he would sire a bunch of kids who would require all his attention, however many it would take: six or eight, maybe even ten.

It turns out real estate agents are always women. They are forty-five years old and feeling restless ever since their children moved out. They can't snoop through their kid's bedrooms any longer, so now they sell real estate and inspect strangers' belongings instead.

Sally finds an agent who's thirty-seven and got restless a little early. She gives the agent a key but hates the whole idea. She worries that some day while she and her poet are tumbling in passion the agent will usher a potential buyer into the bedroom. This could be awkward.

But her fear is unrealistic. Sally can't remember the last time she made love, and she has never discussed anything with her poet except the magazine they intend to publish. They plan to call it *LitCan* in answer to the eternal question, posed by all the English departments in the country: CANLIT?

The magazine will feature his poems and her short stories. Once they create a market for their writing, they will diversify and begin publishing books of his poems, and of her stories. Soon they will be making lots of money. They know their plan is perfect; it can't fail.

Sally cleans up her family heirloom house to make the realtor happy. She polishes the coronation teaspoons, washes and irons the Union Jack over the mantel, discards frayed placemats of Britannia ruling the waves, her cute Queen Elizabeth and Prince Philip salt and pepper shakers, the chipped King George V and Queen Mary teacup. She offers her best junk to the Salvation Army but they refuse it. Apparently they are only interested in the family heirloom furniture she wants to keep. Sally asks them to make an offer, but the Salvation Army has no money so all discussion comes to a halt.

Sally quickly tires of selling her house. As a new topic of conversation it adds pizzazz to coffee breaks but is otherwise unpleasant. Sally is tired of pretending to be neat. She hates picking up her clothes off the floor and stashing them in the laundry basket instead. She is tired of making her bed. It's such a nuisance hiding dirty dishes in the oven.

Friends say that elegance sells. Sally is always broke now from buying fresh flowers for her dyspeptic cat to knock over and chew up. One night it makes a sudden quacking sound. It quacks again. Its eyes bulge like a startled hyperthyroid frog, then it rushes into Sally's cupboard and throws up in a shoe. Sally tries to grab it, but the cat is faster. It moves away, quacks, and throws up in another shoe. She chases it from her cupboard. It rushes onto her family heirloom rug, quacks, throws up again. The cat carefully avoids throwing up in the same place twice. This reminds Sally that fastidiousness was one of the endearing qualities that attracted her to cats in the first place. She stops buying fresh flowers; there's nothing elegant about cat vomit in her shoes.

Just when Sally thinks she can't stand neatness any longer, someone becomes interested in buying her family heirloom house. The real estate agent wants to bring the offer to the office but Sally's too busy to look at it because a time management consultant is watching to see whether she does any work. And unfortunately it's Friday, and she's going to a party straight from the office. The offer expires at midnight. The whole thing is such a nuisance.

They arrange to meet at the party, but the real estate agent arrives late. Sally will have to make a decision quickly because of the midnight deadline. The agent is accompanied by her husband who plans to spend the commission on a yacht club membership. He was daydreaming about this on the way to the party, and got lost. Their Audi could have circled around forever in the one-way streets of Kingston, but a kindly police car led it out. "I felt like poor old Charlie riding around and around underneath Boston,[1]" he tells Sally, and they reminisce about old songs.

Sally has become tired of facing orange juice every morning of her life, so she has been experimenting with Bloody Marys even though she hates the taste of tomato juice, but she has heard it's a good alternative source of vitamin C, and Sally hates catching colds; they're so messy. Cosmopolitan people in Toronto probably drink Bloody Marys for breakfast instead of boring orange juice. Between gulps she sings. "Bloody Mary is the drink I love," trying to convince herself. She wonders what betel nuts look like, and whether she can buy them in Toronto. Surely she must. Love finally conquered all in that old *South Pacific* movie. Before she discovered cocker spaniels, Sally loved Rossano Brazzi and wanted to wash Mitzi Gaynor out of his hair.

Sally knows she'll need extra vitamin C when she moves to Toronto because of smog and pollution, and all the crowds of people coughing on crowded buses and subways.

So now Sally sits on a fire escape mumbling the Bloody Mary song, while on the other side of the open window a bleak punk song was playing. She reads the offer using a tiny flashlight the realtor keeps on her keychain, and then signs her initials wherever she finds an empty space.

She has done it! She has sold the house all her ancestors were raised in! On a fire escape in Kingston, Sally has finally grown up. She's thirty-five years old. It was high time.

Soon the house is back to normal, dirty dishes stacked on the coffee table, and piles of dirty clothes littering the hall floor, sorted according to colour. The phone rings. Sally moves newspapers and potato chip wrappers in a frantic attempt to find it. Then she answers the phone and regrets it. The agent reports a hitch; the buyer has changed his mind.

How can he do this? Sally and her poet need this money to start their magazine.

Before consulting her lawyer, Sally forces down more Bloody Mary vitamin C

Her lawyer is five feet tall. He has sad brown eyes and looks like someone she has seen on TV, Rick Moranis maybe. Sally picked him because of his appearance; she was still attracted to cocker spaniels at the time.

When he sees Sally's piece of paper her lawyer's eyes become even sadder than usual. They are as soppy as blobs of gravy on an heirloom tablecloth. If he has ever been happy his eyes know how to hide it. "You included the purple bedroom drapes and burgundy bedspread? I thought you loved them."

Sally glares. "The buyers adore my colour schemes, Spaniel. They think I should be a decorator or something, because I'm so artistic. They don't want to change a thing."

"How come you didn't throw in your fuzzy orange housecoat and matching cat? They look so good with the apricot living room sheers. And what's this crazy closing date?"

"What else could I do, Spaniel? The buyers didn't know when they would need my house. First they've got to sell the one they already have. They said they'd give me two weeks notice, and were pretty sure it would be this year."

"But you have no idea when you'll have to move."

"No. But anyway, Spaniel, I did it! I sold the house! Aren't you impressed?"

Sally's lawyer munches a handful of antacids from the candy dish on his desk.

"Anyway, Spaniel, that's not why I'm here. They've changed their minds. Can they do that?"

Her lawyer's ears prick up. He reads each page with a magnifying glass. "It's all right," he assures her, patting her hand paternally. "Don't worry. We've got them by the..." and then pauses long enough for Sally to fill in the blanks.

"Is that a leer?" Sally asks. "You really shouldn't try leering, Spaniel. It doesn't suit you."

Worrying comes naturally to Sally. She worries about acid rain and saturated fats and eating red meat. She frets about asbestos insulation, even though she doesn't have any. At the words, Strontium 90, DDT, monosodium glutamate, she gets a cramp inside her gut. Termites might be burrowing inside her walls at this very moment, and white grubs munching beneath her lawn. How would she know?

Mostly she worries that her poet will find someone else who likes his poems.

Sally decides to worry about something else so she won't

have time to think about her house or poet.

Her period is late. Sally doesn't panic. There are good reasons why this could happen. Pregnancy. Menopause at thirty-five. Menopause seems unlikely, and pregnancy even more so; the pill isn't foolproof, but abstinence is.

"Anything worrying you?" her doctor asks.

Sally begins to list them: Strontium 90, cholesterol, acid rain, DDT, nuclear proliferation, drought and famine, the nightly mayhem on TV.... The list is endless and her hormones can't wait it out. She starts bleeding during butylated hydroxytoluene.

That night, at another party, she talks to her friend, Tim. He has cocker spaniel eyes so Sally trusts him. "Watch out," he warns her. "I once tried to sell my house. It took three years. Then the dimwit changed his mind. My lawyer said not to worry; 'You've got him by the short and curlies,' he told me." Sally notices Tim's lawyer is earthier than hers, but Tim's still talking. "Then the other guy's lawyer did a survey and discovered my neighbour's gate swung over my property line by half an inch."

"What did your lawyer say then?" Sally sticks her fingers in her ears so she won't hear his answer all at once.

"He said, 'Whoops. Guess I was wrong. The other guy's got you by yours.' The twit. As if I couldn't feel them being pulled."

Sally considers her crotch. It seems calm as a cantaloupe. No tugging yet.

"The deal fell through, Sally. Be careful." Then he wanders off in search of long-legged greyhound blondes.

Sally wonders how to be careful. Careful means crossing streets at crosswalks, remembering to take the pill, avoiding potato salad at picnics, learning Defendo. None of these seem applicable to her present situation.

Marge traps her in a corner. "Sally! I want to hear all about your new apartment." She has a voice like a braying basset hound.

"Shh, Marge. It's a secret." Sally frantically checks the room for all the men who look like Rick Moranis. There are dozens of them and any one might be her lawyer. Without her glasses she can't tell. "I don't want my lawyer to know I've already signed a lease. He gets upset whenever I sign papers he hasn't had a chance to change. He keeps trying to look after me. He's such a frustrated father figure. He needs someone to take care of."

Marge chokes on a chocolate-covered pretzel. "You've still got that same lawyer? That child you used to go out with?"

"Yeah. But now he's almost thirty and acts a whole lot older. He's so old-fashioned he still drinks them."

"Hm?"

"Old-fashioneds." Sally sips her Bloody Mary. "We're just friends now. The romance thing ended. I still can't understand it. I thought I would love his spaniel eyes forever. Anyway, he says I've got it made selling the house. If the deal falls through I just tuck the down payment in my bra and start again."

"He actually said that? Putting money inside your bra? He thinks you still wear one?"

"A direct quote. That's the way he talks. It's sort of quaint."

"Keeping the money and starting again sounds good. All you lose is a bit of time."

"Yeah, but…"

"But?"

"Well, I met this sweetheart of a poet and we intend to start up a magazine. You should see him. He looks like a shaggy sheepdog and his poems blow my mind. I've already signed a lease in Toronto."

"Toronto! You didn't tell me the apartment's in Toronto! Where they have muggings in supermarket line-ups and at the communion table in church? Sally! You can't mean it!"

Marge's voice reaches every corner of the room. Olives are choked on. Flirtations stop mid-wink. Assignations stop mid-motel-room-key. Sally, good old limestone-Kingston Sally, intends to move down the lonesome 401 to cold Toronto.

Everyone knows how to handle hearing something they are

not supposed to know. They chatter. Spaniels and greyhound blondes chatter like squirrels. They nibble on nuts; their beady eyes look elsewhere; they are pretending to be deaf.

The only spaniel who doesn't pretend is her lawyer. "Sally! You can't move to Toronto. You've got responsibilities. A family heirloom house with a deal that's falling through. You've got a lawyer to support."

Sally wonders how she ever found him appealing; his eyes are moist and pleading. The wrinkles on his forehead seem so vulnerable that she has to look away.

Sally pats him on the head. "Goodbye forever, Spaniel," she tells him. "Sell the house. Fax the papers to Toronto so I can sign them."

Sally grabs her coat and leaves. She jaywalks and crosses against red lights, picks up potato salad at a sleazy deli. Life is risky.

She is thinking of her poet, his poems, his sheepdog hair. She wonders what colour his eyes are. It's good to know she'll never have to see them.

---

[1]The man who never returned.

Long Point

THERE ARE NO WORDS INSIDE her head. Doreen just keeps driving through the sweltering heat. She passes fields of orange pumpkins, drifting past them easily. They could be beach balls on an ocean. She would like to be beside an ocean right now. Or anywhere else.

She passes a sign, the turnoff to Long Point. She has never even seen Lake Erie. How often has she mentioned this to Earl? "We live so close. Let's drive down and see what it looks like...." Why did she bother because she already knew his answer? "Nah. You've seen one lake, you've seen them all."

Lake water washes over Doreen's mind like a cool blue dream, then flows into a deep depression in the earth. Fish swim inside that lake; boats float on top; seagulls flick back and forth stringing their white hieroglyphs on the blue sky. Waves roll against the shore, rearranging sand and pebbles, washing up treasures: driftwood, bits of coloured glass....

She remembers a line from a poem, imperfectly, but it doesn't matter: "Men at forty close doors to rooms they won't return to."[1]

Doreen swerves to a sudden stop at the side of the highway, in a flurry of gravel, and a prolonged blare of the horn from the car behind her. The driver gives her the finger, and Doreen gives it right back. She makes a sudden U-turn and heads south toward the lake.

The road is empty. People are already huddled around kitchen tables making attempts at conversation: "Pass the peas." "Any more meat?" "What's for dessert?"

Fields of tobacco border the road, with their small neat curing sheds, like the little frame cottages by Cape Cod Bay. Once Doreen stayed in a cabin near Provincetown. She lay beside a sweet boy named Nicky for three days and nights, their bodies slick with sweat, the salt air fecund and heavy. Nothing existed beyond the cabin walls. They lay on sandy sheets on a lumpy mattress that smelled as though mice were living inside, but these things didn't matter. They made love again and again, and knew this was the reason they had been placed upon the earth.

Ladders lean against the tobacco sheds. Doreen could climb a ladder, hide inside, and pretend to be that twenty-year-old again.

Painting less and less. When did she finally stop? Give up on her dreams of New York, London, Paris? Settle for whatever she could easily get: A nothing life in a falling-down house in a backwater town? Teaching kindergarten kids who don't want to be at school? Drinking at the Legion every Saturday night?

Earl.

She'd seen the sign from two blocks away and instantly realized what it was, imagining the entire rowdy scenario: Earl and his buddies spending all afternoon at the Legion, joking with the guy at the gas station on the way home, talking him into letting them borrow the sign for the night, heaving it into the back of the pick-up. Earl driving slow around the corners, as the guys in the back braced themselves against the sign to keep it steady until they reached the house. Then one guy in the truck shoving the sign down to Earl and the others. Them wrestling it into position in the front yard where the late September grass had already turned from green to straw. The guys boisterous, horsing around, making the usual sexual comments: "What about you, Earl? Getting old, too?" His rooster strut: "Nope I still get it up and it stays there. This stud doesn't need any Viagra."

Doreen drove past, fast, eyes straight ahead, trying to avoid the light-bulb message: LORDY, LORDY. GUESS WHO JUST TURNED FORTY?

Not her name, though. At least she's grateful for that. No DOREEN in capital letters, but it doesn't matter. Everyone knows. Old ladies peering through lace curtains, children jostling on the school bus, delivery truck drivers, the town cops in their patrol car, the mailman, old guys tossing flyers onto porches. Everyone can answer the illuminated question. "Guess who? That's easy. Doreen."

Sweat pours out of her body as though it's glad to get away. The car radio announces a record high for the end of September: ninety-one degrees. They also mention the centigrade temperature, but Doreen doesn't pay attention. She's never bothered making the transition. Unseasonable though. Unbearably hot. Probably this is what hot flashes are like.

Forty. 40. XL. Arabic or Roman it doesn't matter; the meaning's the same. XL: extra large, too much. Journalists place thirty at the end of an article to indicate that the story's over. Forty is even worse.

Birds line the wires along the road, dark silhouettes against the sky. It is almost October and they are gathering, getting ready to move on. She once read a novel in which a character didn't believe in migration, as if her opinion mattered, as though migration disappears if one doesn't believe in it, the way God does. The woman claimed that birds stay in Canada for the winter and freeze to death.[2] A painful thought. Something else for Doreen to try to erase from her mind. Like Earl. She doesn't intend to think about him.

Doreen pulls into a gas station and buys a take-out coffee. She starts to drive away, then changes her mind and pulls up beside the phone booth. Earl shouts, "Are you okay? For God's sake where are you?" She can hear loud music in the background, and hollering voices.

"I'm fine. I just needed to be alone."

"Alone? You want to be all alone? Without me? Without our friends? But it's your birthday! Everyone's here! I already ordered your favourite pizza. Charlie even brought over some Mexican beer. It's got a name like the dishes: Corella or something."

"I'm sorry."

"Sorry? What good is that? We're having a party here. Rose made a triple layer chocolate cake with coloured sprinkles. She put forty birthday candles on top! What the hell are we going to do about that cake? Are we supposed to eat it or not?"

"I don't care. Do whatever you want. She can blow out forty candle flames herself, or let them burn down and melt the coloured sprinkles. I think our fire insurance is paid up."

"Geez, Doreen. You must be crazy. Rose baked you a beautiful cake. Just a sec. I'll put her on the line so you can thank her."

"No. Someone's waiting for this phone. I've got to go. I'll call you tomorrow."

"Tomorrow? What's going on? Where the hell are you?"

Doreen hangs up, muttering "Dammit, dammit, dammit," mad at herself for everything: for phoning him up, driving past the house, ever getting involved with him in the first place. She speeds up, driving too fast down the gravel road, sipping her bitter coffee, spilling some on her skirt, giving herself something else to complain about. "Dammit, dammit."

She sees a sign beside an inlet: CABINS FOR RENT.

"Don't you want to see the cabin first?" the guy asks. "My wife calls it Elsie." As if she cares whether the cabin has a name. "No. It doesn't matter. I'll only be here one night."

As she opens the cabin door a wind chime jiggles: small ceramic cows clink against each other. On a wallpaper border by the ceiling, Holsteins march around the room, a stark black and white monochrome, except for their enormous shocking-pink udders. Cow magnets fasten the rental rates to the fridge.

Doreen hangs her jacket on a cow coat rack, checks the cow

cookie jar on the counter, but it's empty, so she opens the curtains and looks outside. Maybe the scenery will rest her eyes. Good. Water. No fields of cattle.

Cobwebs cover the outside of the window. All the same a huge spider weaves more silk back and forth. A big fly buzzes loud, louder, struggling to get free. Doreen mutters, "Give up. You've had it," but then watches it pull free of the sticky strands and fly off erratically. It actually escapes. She can hardly believe her eyes. It seems like an omen.

Beyond the window is a hummock of goldenrod, tall grasses, Queen Anne's lace, and then a marsh alive with birds. Wooden posts stick up from the water, each with a seagull huddled on top, facing into the wind. Canada geese are the only other birds she recognizes. An assortment of ducks. If she had a bird book she could try to tell them apart. It would give her a reason to be here.

She stares at the open water beyond the marsh. How far can she see? Miles. If she had binoculars she could see even farther. Then she notices two white shapes. What? Can they really be? She can hardly believe it: a pair of swans.

Swans! She has never seen wild ones before; their silhouettes stark against the water, crisp as paper cutouts on a background of blue cardboard. Unreal, as though they've been set in place by a surrealist painter, or have appeared inside a dream. Perhaps she *has* dreamed them. She squeezes her eyes shut, opens them again. Nope. Still there.

They are so beautiful. Doreen could watch these swans forever. She could spend the rest of her life here, learning the names of all these water birds that twitter and grack and peep and screech above the marsh.

If she was independently wealthy. If she could afford to spend her days gazing at birds instead of teaching kindergarten. If Earl could find a steady job. If they didn't need to eat.

Suddenly she is hungry, starving. She needs groceries: beer, instant coffee, bread and cheese, bananas, a toothbrush. She remembers passing a sign to some town, Port something or other, and drives there slowly, studying everything, memorizing. Port Rowan.

In a park she sees a historical plaque: "The Heroine of Long Point," and thinks this is someone she can identify with. Having just avoided a birthday bash with Earl and his boozy buddies she feels like a heroine herself, but then reads the plaque and is diminished.

> In November 1854, the schooner "Conductor" was wrecked off this shore during one of Lake Erie's many violent storms. Jeremiah Becker, who resided nearby, was away on the mainland but his courageous wife, Abigail, risked her life by repeatedly entering the water to assist the exhausted seamen to shore. The eight sailors were housed and fed in her cabin until they recovered from their ordeal....

When she returns to the cabin and flops down on the couch, the smell of cat pee surrounds her, so she moves onto the cob-webbed porch instead, eating her bread and cheese, drinking beer, watching for swans, as light disappears from the sky and lake. But the swans don't return, and she keeps thinking of Leda, the Yeats poem, the thrashing wings.[3]

She can't sleep. Rustling sounds are everywhere: beyond her window, beneath the floorboards, behind the walls. The roof creaks, as though someone is walking on it. At six a.m. she is up drinking instant coffee on the porch, gazing at the grey water and the grey skies above.

Then suddenly, the clouds are tinged with gold as the sun moves up behind them. Doreen imagines a medieval painter working with gold leaf, licking a glistening paintbrush, then gilding the edges of the clouds. The artist gazes at his painting of that sky and its reflection in the lake, smiling, satisfied, unaware of the poison slowly working inside him.

The pond is silent, smooth as a pane of glass, but suddenly a circle appears on the surface and widens to several feet. Then another, and another. Perhaps raindrops are falling, or insects landing on the pond. She goes closer to investigate. No.

But the circles keep widening, faster and faster, dozens of them now, moving outward and intersecting. Doreen hears a plopping sound and a splash. She peers down into murky green water but can't see any fish. Maybe clams are moving, turning over, stretching, then once again burying themselves deep inside soft mud, like that original muck we all emerged from.

Life proceeds according to some pattern. Doreen needs to believe this. Strange things keep happening, but the universe knows what it's doing. Circles have always appeared on this water and will continue long after she has gone. She doesn't need to understand this or take any responsibility.

The sun finally breaks free of the horizon. Sky and water are suddenly too bright for Doreen's eyes and she turns away and notices a dust cloud following a transport truck along the gravel road, then flashing lights, and a splash of bright yellow as a school bus stops to pick up children.

Oh no! Today is Tuesday; people are living their ordinary lives, and the cycles of industry and education carry on. She should have thought to phone in sick! The principal's secretary will have phoned in a panic, and what in the world would Earl have told her?

A duck glides on the water. Doreen pictures his feet paddling up and down beneath the surface to make this happen. So much that takes place is invisible. Lily pads float on the water like flattened hearts.

Probably she would have left him anyway, sooner or later, when she was brave enough.

The wind is rising and tall grasses wave to and fro. Poplar leaves rustle above her head, a shushing sound like a lullaby, almost soothing her back to sleep. When the swans finally appear she feels brave enough to phone Earl.

He starts hollering, "Where in the world are you? I waited up all night. Is it hormones? PMS? Menopause? Can you get it this early?"

"At forty? Maybe. I feel old enough today. Like my tissues are drying up and fading. I'm not ready for this to happen. Maybe no one is ever ready, but it doesn't seem fair. I haven't even lived yet. I've never had a kid. I haven't done anything I meant to, and dammit, now I'm forty and it's too late."

"I thought you were happy. I thought I was enough. You said you loved me."

"Oh, Earl, it's got nothing to do with you. It's a birthday thing, a milestone crisis. You know how you suddenly stop every once in a while and wonder what you're doing, where you're going with your life?"

"Nope. I've made my choices. I know where my life is at."

"Well, great. I'm happy for you."

"Are you being sarcastic?"

"Yep. Guess so. Anyway, I've got to go." Doreen hangs up fast, but not fast enough. She hears Earl's protesting, "But..."

She returns to the porch. The swans still glide on blue water, and the marsh is alive with movement, with twitters and squawks, but the magic is gone. She grabs a notebook and starts to write. "Dear Earl. It is so easy to close doors behind you, and so hard." Now what? What comes next? She rips the page out and scrunches it up, then climbs in a car and drives back to the park in Port Rowan, to study the historical plaque.

She calculates: Abigail Becker was only twenty-four years old at the time, and experiencing the high point of her life. Afterward how could she ever cope with her day-to-day life? But pioneer women were always performing superhuman feats, just the effort of existence, of raising a family while always threatened by plagues or natural disasters. She lived. She was a survivor. She saw what needed to be done, and then did it. She was a heroine all right. She didn't run away.

Doreen makes another instant coffee and plunks it on the floor of the porch. She intends to sit quietly and absorb this scene so she will never forget it. Memorizing the sounds, the creak of her rocker against the floorboards, the plop of bubbles on the surface of the water, all the splashes and screeches and rustling she cannot possibly identify.

A man comes by and feeds the fish. He says he does this every day. "Want to see some carp? I throw them a bit of cooked meat everyday. They're bottom-feeders, them and the dogfish. Just staying down there at the bottom, their mouths waiting for whatever drifts down."

A pause, then, "Want to tell terns from gulls? Throw some bread out. Gulls are the ones that come. And their sounds are different; terns sound like cat fights." Doreen doesn't answer, and he finally leaves.

Doreen peers into the water and sees nothing. But the carp are there, ordinary, reliable, staying where they belong. Living their boring carp lives, eating and being eaten, part of the food chain.

Swans float above them, not better, of course, but beautiful. Doreen once dreamed of becoming one; as a child she had heard her mother read that ugly duckling story too often.

And then, oh my God! Earl's buddy knows how to trace phone calls! Earl will be able to find her. She packs up fast and writes a note:

Dear Earl,

I'm sorry. It is so easy to close doors behind us, and so hard. A poet named Donald Justice says people at forty close doors to rooms they won't return to.[1] He has been there and should know. Bolder folks probably slam them. We timid folks close them gently, hoping no one will notice, worrying whether the latch will hold, or whether that door will keep swinging to and fro like a saloon door in a western movie. And whether we'll keep swinging back

*and forth ourselves. But we have to do something. It's been
driving us crazy, knowing other rooms are waiting to be
explored.*
      Some day I may regret this.

Doreen closes the door and returns the key. She has no idea
where she's going, dragging along forty years of baggage,
cobweb memories of one small town after another, Earl, old
daydreams of someone she might turn into. She would like
to discard those daydreams, stash them into a trash barrel at
some gas station along the way. A sleeping bag or change of
clothes would be more useful.

If she bought some watercolours perhaps she could turn her
daydreams into strange surreal paintings. If she had paper
and a paintbrush. If she remembers how to dip the brush into
water and paint, and how to translate that paint into shapes
that seem to have meaning. She is talking to herself, trying to
remember how to do this, trying to reteach herself, novice,
little kindergarten kid.

And now Doreen is shouting, above the noise of the speeding tires on crushed gravel, above a twangy lonesome radio
song. She notices a road sign: #3 A HERITAGE HIGHWAY and
hollers, "Of course. Like all the paths we travel." She pauses,
then adds, "So what?"

[1] Donald Justice. "Men at forty learn to close softly the doors to rooms
they will not be coming back to." *Selected Poems* (Atheneum, 1979).
[2] Helen Humphreys. *Ethel on Fire* (Black Moss Press, 1991).
[3] William Butler Yeats. "Leda and the Swan." *The Poems of W. B.
Yeats* (Collier Books, 1989).

Luv: A Librarian Fantasy

MEN CALL CLARA *LUV* THESE DAYS. It seems to be a fashion. Regulars at the library say "Hi, Luv," when they enter, and, "Thanks, Luv," when they leave. Only the men. Each time a man says luv to her she wants to love him back.

She fantasizes all the time.

The town planner's voice is gentle. "Hey, Luv. Are you busy? I'm looking for a history book about the city."

"I'm coming," Clara says, and knows this won't be an ordinary search; she has always been a sucker for urban affairs.

Sunlight streams toward them from a skylight. CBC radio is playing background music, a Brandenberg concerto. Customers are quietly browsing. Afterward, Clara wants to remember which Brandenberg was playing. She hums it to people as they check out their books but no one knows.

On her lunch hour, Clara hums it in a record shop, but the guy behind the counter doesn't recognize it; he had no idea that music existed before New Wave. He says, "Never mind, Luv. I'll play you something else," and he does.

A man is glancing through a poetry book. "That's my favourite poet," she mentions.

"Which poem do you like best, Luv?" he asks, and then recites it as Clara holds onto the counter for support. "What time do you get off work, Luv? I'll be waiting in the park to tell you more poems." He brings a blanket, a bottle of wine.

"You forgot the book," Clara mentions.

"It doesn't matter, Luv," he says, "I know them all by heart," and then begins, "How do I luv thee."[1]

Errands are exhausting. The guy at the fruit market says, "Hi, Luv," and touches her breasts. "Like ripe peaches," he tells her, then starts to suck.

"Hi, Luv," says the butcher, then folds her clothes and places them neatly on the counter. "You don't want sawdust on these," he cautions, being thoughtful.

They all think her name is Luv, these men she runs into at the cleaners, the post office, the bakery, in the line-up at the bank machine. By the time Clara gets to her apartment she is exhausted. A tenant is unlocking his door as she comes along the hall. "Rough day?" he asks. "Yeah. I'm going to lie down and have a rest."

"Good idea, Luv," he says. Later they make supper.

---

[1]Elizabeth Barrett Browning. *Sonnets from the Portuguese* (1850).

Marking Time

HANNAH KEEPS GETTING OLDER all the time. How does this happen? she wonders, because surely she is in her prime, now, right this minute. She still feels she is in the middle of her life. She has always felt this way.

Hannah is fifteen; her childhood a burden she drags behind her, like her little sisters, hoping to shed. She waits for the next stage, because surely it will be better. Her future stretches ahead, like a field of snow, untrodden and endless. She might live until she's as old as thirty. Well, of course, she can't imagine living to thirty, but most people do survive that long. What in the world will it feel like, being so ancient, being mature? She wonders whether other people can picture how their lives will go. Is she the only person who can't do this? Lacking some part of the brain that would be capable of such imagination? Another lack to add to all the others: small breasts, shyness, absence of original thoughts that would stun others with their insight. Hannah is fifteen years old and mostly missing. She consists of absences and lacks, but is always hopeful; surely being grown-up will be better.

Hannah is nineteen, and no longer pregnant, but at the moment still barefoot. A baby is always propped on her hip or tugging at her breast. The freshly mown grass in the park stains her bare feet, and surrounds her with such a sweet scent she wants to cry. These are the best moments of her life, she thinks. They must be, because she feels so good, being needed

by an infant, needing that infant right back, an instinctive sym-
biosis, both of them helpless in the face of this overwhelming
love, this need to suckle and be sucked on, to be clutched and
to hang on tight, inhaling each other's breath.

Her previous life was only a preamble. Everything led toward
this moment; whatever follows can only be an anticlimax. A
baby exists and needs to be held, so Hannah holds it. Pretty
soon the baby will turn into a toddler and keep growing older,
but it won't matter because another baby will have already
replaced it. These babies have a father, of course. Gus appears
each evening to eat supper and discuss the boring details of
his day. Each morning he disappears, from Hannah's presence,
from her mind. Eventually he disappears forever. Later she will
try to remember which day it was, which year.

Hannah turns fifty. Half a century! Imagine! The babies
have grown up long ago and moved far away somewhere or
other, each one at the centre of her own life, as Hannah arrives
at this milestone of hers. Half a century! Can it be possible?
Has she stored away fifty years of memories and snapshots?
Accumulated enough knowledge to see her through? Acquired
a bit of wisdom? Of course not. Is this what fifty is like, then?
This lack of sufficient memories and knowledge? Only for
me, Hannah thinks. Probably other people have somehow
assimilated, learned, matured. All the same, she continues
to feel she is at the middle of her life, ignoring the ridiculous
mathematics; surely she still has lots of time, time for something else, whatever.

Hannah is sixty. Really? How did it happen? She stares at
a stranger's body in the mirror, the sags, the wrinkles, and
blemishes. She wants her own body back. This time she will
appreciate it. She bargains, in case some god or goddess is out
there. (Surely there must be something!) She promises to do
whatever it wants, to relive her past and make changes. Just
tell me how far back you want me to go, she tells it, but then
remembers fifteen. No, please not those teen years again. That

enormous lack, while unaware just how much was missing. Not fifteen, but maybe thirty. She would appreciate thirty.

What is she thinking? She would love any earlier age. Thirty, forty, even fifty . Just not this age, whatever it is, because it keeps increasing as she bargains. Can she really be sixty already? Or is it seventy? And still growing even older? While always daydreaming of being younger.

Hannah is into denial these days, or perhaps she is simply learning how to lie. "I feel great," she tells everyone, and imagines their comments later: "Isn't she amazing? She seems so young and energetic!" Surely people must say this to each other. She certainly hopes so.

Hannah keeps on growing older; it seems to be happening faster and faster. She is ancient now, and calmly, objectively, considering death. But she worries about the dying process that precedes it, and tries to imagine what it will be like. Serene, she hopes, a simple letting go, like the way she drifts into sleep at night. But she watched her parents breathe their last, and it wasn't beautiful at all. She would like to die in her sleep.

Each night Hannah slips peacefully into sleep, but then the nightmares take over, of intractable pain, of struggling for breath, as death, that ruthless intruder, squeezes her neck tighter and tighter, until she wakes up in a panic, covered in sweat.

She thinks of that grotesque little hangman game she played with Jill and Jessie when they were little. Them laughing as the body appeared and acquired arms and legs, all the while dangling from the gallows.

By the time she is fully awake she has forgotten the nightmare, and once again hopes to die in her sleep, when no one is watching or trying to intervene. She is ready now. Let's just get it over with, she mutters. If she were religious she would pray, asking the Almighty to hurry up about it.

But suddenly her children aren't ready to let her go. They are grown-up now, of course. They left home at twenty and have ignored her as much as possible ever since, involved with careers, spouses, children of their own. Busy, always busy. Juggling all their activities: gardening, jogging, curling, adultery, whatever.

Jill and Jessie used to travel; they would plop a grandchild on her lap, and expect her to be delighted. She still remembers what that was like.

A grandson skipping along beside her. "Slow down," she tells him. "For heaven's sake, slow down!" Doesn't he realize he could knock her over? She's so frail now since her latest fall, walking slowly, even with her cane. Tottering. Fragile. Would another fall kill her? Or break her hip? Keep her flat on her back until she succumbed to a blood clot or pneumonia?

"Not so fast," she tells him. "The world is round you know. We have to walk slowly so we don't fall off."

He laughs. "Round like a ball?"

"That's right."

"I don't care. I'm a big boy now. I won't fall off."

"But I might." She grabs his hand and holds on tight. Then they continue toward the park, walking slowly, holding hands.

Grandchildren. She knows there were some, but lately she can't remember their names or what they look like. Of course not. Sometimes she doesn't remember her children's names either, so she keeps them written on a notepad by the kitchen phone. But today she doesn't need a reminder. She says the words over and over, practising so she won't forget them again: Jill and Jessie, Jill and Jessie, Jill and Jessie.... She needs to ask them something. What happened to my nice little apartment? Where's my rocking chair? Where are all my pretty trinkets?

Her daughters have been growing older, too; they have regrets and yearnings and questions of their own. Jill needs to learn her ancestry; Jessie wants to discover the meaning of life, and suspects they're the same thing.

It is not easy to be this old, Hannah thinks; just wait until they try it, then they'll understand. She is always exhausted. Everything takes so much energy: struggling up out of her chair, tottering to the bathroom, eating meals that arrive three times a day whether she's hungry or not. Whether she even likes the food. Sometimes just sitting still and breathing tires her out. All that energy that once bubbled inside her seems to have disappeared.

Where did it go? she wonders, but then remembers raising her children and knows Jill and Jessie used it up. It must be their fault.

Or maybe her blood is thinner and doesn't contain all the ingredients her body needs. Perhaps it lacks something essential: blood cells or plasma, haemoglobin, whatever. Or perhaps her heart, that sweet dependable old muscle, has finally worn out, exhausted from pushing all that blood around. Built-in obsolescence, Hannah thinks. Car manufacturers didn't invent it after all; they learned by observing their own bodies. Uphill to twenty or twenty-five, then downhill, sliding downhill all the way, speeding fast, then faster, faster.

She and Gus didn't trade in their old car. They bought it used in the first place, and drove it until it was ready for the scrap heap. Then they towed it to a wrecker's, removed the license plates, and walked away without glancing back. This place she's in reminds her of those scrap yards.

Hannah remembers a school poem about a one-horse shay,[1] each part built just as strong as every other, so that everything finally broke down at the same time. She wants to suddenly collapse like that. She waits and waits but that's not the way it happens.

Instead her thoughts, her sentences, deteriorate. All her stories.... Whatever happened to all those stories she used to tell? They dwindled down to paragraphs, then disjointed sentences, and now have disintegrated into mere fragments: "Oh well..." "I only mean..." "Isn't it...?" "Oh, dear."

It is driving her children crazy, happening now, at the wrong time. As if there could ever have been a perfect moment.

Jill has suddenly realized that her mother will disappear, taking all her memories with her. Stories of her childhood, parents and grandparents, aunts and uncles. Jill has distant relatives out there somewhere and doesn't even know their names. And what was the world like when her mother was growing up? Jill can't imagine it at all. No TV, no smart phones, no internet. Her mother lived through the aftermath of a depression, then World War II and the cold war, the space race, Korea, Vietnam.... She has seen everything change, then keep on changing. She used to prattle about the old days, the old breakable seventy-eight records, the pedestal phones. Before plastics and antibiotics and pop-up toasters. Before microwave ovens. It sounded ancient and boring, so Jill hadn't paid attention. Of course not. Why would she? Because her mother's voice was constant; it never stopped. A persistent background of white noise, like the hum of insects. It droned around her daughters while their minds drifted elsewhere. It seemed as though their mother's voice would go on forever. Now Jill needs to hear those stories again; she wants to riffle through her mother's memories, like pages of an old history book. This time she will finally pay attention and write everything down.

And Jessie is having some kind of crisis. She has no idea what to call it. Not mid-life anyway, unless she plans to live to be nearly a hundred, and she certainly doesn't intend to do that. But lately she has begun to ponder the meaning of existence, and wonders why it has taken her so long. She borrows philosophy books from the library but can't understand them. Ma has lived for more than eighty years and must have learned things that are important. She should have told Jessie whatever she'd discovered. This should have happened years ago. Surely parents have a responsibility to pass on wisdom.

Hannah hears them grumble "Dammit," whenever they ask a question and her answer doesn't please them. She is doing the best she can. Her children have always demanded too much. "Dammit," one of them mutters again.

"What does it all mean?" some woman asks. Is she talking to her? Hannah sighs and opens her eyes, sees someone too close, staring into her face. Is it Momma? Surely not. It looks a bit like her, though. Except for the eyes. Even with the cancer, Momma's eyes were never watery like that.

"What does it all mean?" As if Hannah has ever figured out what life is all about. As if she can possibly know the answer. Who is asking her such a dumb question? A daughter? How many are there, anyway? Only two? She can't remember. Hasn't she already done enough for those children? and answers herself aloud, "No, probably not."

"What did she say?" a voice asks.

"I'm not sure. Blobbity blah. Something like that. I couldn't understand her."

"None of your business," Hannah mumbles. "I wasn't talking to you anyway," and then her mind moves somewhere else.

She's thirsty, opens her eyes. Is water boiling on the stove? Perhaps to make a pot of tea?

"Tea." There. She's said it.

"Oh good. She's awake. Hi there, Ma. We've been waiting for you to wake up."

"Mmmm…"

"C'mon, Ma. It's me, Jill. I've got the picture album." She holds it up. "Here it is. See?"

As though I don't know a picture album when I see one, Hannah thinks. Anyway, it's mine. What is she doing snooping through it? Trying to discover all my secrets?

"I want to put names on the back of each picture so Jessie and I will know who the people are. I'll show them to you one at a time and write the names on the back. Okay?"

Hannah remembers something. "Tea."

"Tea? You want tea right now? Maybe we could look at some pictures first. Then we can stop for a cup of tea and take a rest…"

"Tea…"

"Okay, okay. I guess I can find you a cup of tea. I won't be long."

Hannah wanders back in time. She is in some different body, that of a little child. Her parents are alive again and telling her something they think is important: "Eat up your vegetables. Eat lots of carrots so you can see in the dark." Sometimes they talk quietly and she can't understand them. "Little pitchers have big ears." Little Hannah stares at photos on the wall, but the ears seem the same as always.

A voice is saying something. "Okay, Ma. Here's your tea. Let me help you, so it doesn't spill."

Hannah lets go of childhood, is back inside her scrawny old-woman body again. Dammit. Someone wants her to drink a cup of tea. The woman keeps insisting, as if it matters, as if the tea can't wait until later. Hannah scrunches her eyes shut. If they think she's asleep then perhaps they'll leave her alone. She doesn't want to drink tea of all things. Not today. She feels too hot. Lemonade, maybe. Or gin. She remembers hot summers, a rocking chair on a shady porch. A nice fizzy gin and tonic to quench her thirst. Ice clicking against the glass, that tinkling sleigh-bell sound.

The voice keeps yattering on and on.

"I've got to leave. Dammit, Jessie, I'm so disappointed. I've been here all day and she only woke up once and then asked for this stupid cup of tea. I want to put names on these snapshots. Try to get some of them done if she wakes up."

Voices buzzing, far away, like flies throwing themselves against a screen, or stuck on sticky paper near the ceiling. *Bzzz, bzzz, bzzz.* These people keep bothering her. Who are they? Why don't they go away?

"I wanted to label these photos. I need to know who these people are."

Another voice. "Too late now. Way too late."

I want, I want, like those grandkids used to say. "I want Grandma to read me a story. I want her to make me ginger-bread cookies."

I want, I want. And what about me? Hannah thinks. What

had I wanted? Too much. The moon and stars. A perfect fairy-tale romance. Someone, anyone, to marry her so she could leave Momma and Papa far behind. She had daydreamed all the time, imagining some nice young man who resembled Gus but was more exciting.

"Ma! Hey, Ma, wake up! I've got to leave. Dammit!"

"Maybe Aunt Patsy will know who they are."

"Fat chance. Anyway, we never see her. I don't even know where she is."

"Or maybe Daddy..."

"Yeah? He can't even remember how to use a knife and fork. Anyway, these snapshots are mostly from Ma's side of the family."

So Gus will finally defeat her, wherever he is. Is he still at home? Or in some old-age place like this one? Apparently he's going to live longer. Well, why not? He had a cushy desk job. So him outliving her doesn't really count. Hannah hopes he knows it.

He didn't run around after children all day long; probably chased leggy secretaries instead. Hannah was always taking care of Momma, because her sisters always lived somewhere else and she never knew where to find them. She was always so worn down by pregnancies and miscarriages, and by her sweet little infants needing to be suckled and shushed in the middle of the night. By toddlers needing to be cuddled and chased after and grabbed and kept safe. To be taught to behave, how to tie shoelaces, how to tell time.

Her sweet little daughters, Jill and Jessie. And wasn't there another one who died? Maybe. She isn't sure.

Hannah tries to remember not being tired, but that memory seems to be missing. All that laundering, scrubbing, cooking, preserving. When will it ever end? She had wondered, and had imagined what that final ending would be like, that peaceful moment, breathing her last. Stretched out in her best dress, wearing new stockings without runs or snags, the trace of a smile hovering about her face, as she prepares to laze about the clouds and do nothing, forever, throughout all of eternity. Little children being shushed, held up in their parents' arms, smiling down at her on the bed. "Look at Granny..., Great-granny. Doesn't she look nice? She's going up to heaven to visit the angels. It's lovely there. That's why she's smiling."

"Dammit," Hannah mumbles. "It isn't beautiful at all." Her eyes scrunched shut because of the glare of the overhead light, her skin scraped raw by the rough starchy hospital nightgown and sheets. And now a bell keeps ringing. Is she in church? And someone pokes a needle into her arm, hard, again and again, searching for a vein, then finally shoves the needle directly into her heart.

We are born in pain, and leave in pain. Hannah once read this somewhere. It seems to be true.

---

[1] Oliver Wendell Holmes. *The Deacon's Masterpiece, or The Wonderful One-hoss Shay* (Houghton Mifflin, 1895).

[2] "For we are born in other's pain/ And perish in our own." Francis Thompson. "Daisy, Stage 15." *Modern British Poetry* (1920).

Meat Market

BARS ARE WHERE IT ALWAYS HAPPENS, but she's fed up now and getting stronger.

Another night, a different bar, some other guy. Music so loud he can't hear what she's saying.

"I always end up falling for men like you. I never learn. You guys always seems so sweet and attentive, smiling as though you mean it, laugh lines crinkled around your eyes. Maintaining eye contact all the time, like you really care about what I'm saying. Your eyes never wander away from mine. They don't need to. You have them trained; they won't betray you.

"You say nothing, but it doesn't matter. I know the thoughts I want you to have, and imagine them inside your mind. I make you up into the kind of guy I can fall for, and then I do.

"You seem so sweet and safe, the kind of guy I've always been waiting for, the one who will try to understand me, who'll really care. Someone I can trust with all my secrets. A prince, like that guy who woke up Cinderella, or maybe Snow White.

"Men like you belong in fairy tales. Or inside a kid's activity book: connect the dots, see who you get.

"I daydream about guys like you, ones I've imagined. I always have to make you up, because you are silent and tell me nothing, while I babble on and on to fill in all those empty gaps. I think I know you, but only know some storybook fantasy I've told myself. You're really not there at all, but time goes by before I realize."

He lifts her chin, brushes her hair away from her face so he can maintain eye contact better.

"I once lived with a man like you. It wasn't sudden. We'd been seeing each other for a couple of years; we'd shared all our ambitions and thoughts and dreams. I say we, but I'm really referring to myself. I told him all my dreams of what our life together would be like, and he smiled his sweet smile and rubbed his hand against my cheek. I thought it meant that he agreed.

"I told him how much I wanted us to move away. He was in the middle of some project, so I knew I'd have to wait until it was finished. But when the time came it turned out he had a million reasons why he couldn't budge. Do you suppose he knew that all along? Do you think he intended to trick me?

"I don't think so. I think he was never listening. I think he had learned how to look sincere and interested while his mind drifted somewhere else, wherever the wind blew.

"You even look like him a little.

"I've tried to like men who are different and talk a lot. They don't listen, either, because I can't slip a word in edgewise. They want to tell their own stories, and have them handy: push a button and a tape starts playing: Anecdote 27: *The first time I met the Red Sox goalie he'd been drinking too much beer....* Pathetic Memoir 35: *When I was five my daddy backed the car over my puppy....* I want to holler to stop the machine and erase that tape. I've heard it too many times already, but my folks raised me to be polite."

He keeps stroking her hand and gazing into her eyes, while rehearsing the PowerPoint presentation for tomorrow's board meeting. It's going to knock them dead.

"You're the kind of guy who won't be faithful, who'll con one woman after another, the way you're trying to con me right now. You won't admit it if I ask you. Of course not. You speak, but never say anything that matters. Just yatter on and on, bumping your gums together: *The guy came back with three and a quarter but we both knew he'd go higher....* All you corporate guys talk like that. The same way my Momma prattled about her bridge games: *When I played my five of diamonds, Lucy Babble knew what I meant....* Filling up silence but saying nothing.

"You're the kind of guy I warn my friends against, that we tell our shrinks about: *But he's such a nice guy, a sweetheart; he always seems to pay attention....* The shrink makes his usual soothing *Mmmm hmmm* sounds and we suspect he's not listening either.

"You're nothing but trouble with a capital T."

He smiles sympathetically whenever her conversation falters. It always works.

"I once had a breakdown because of a guy like you."

He hasn't moved on her too fast, hasn't done anything to offend her. That's why he can't believe it when she slaps his face, strides to the door, and slams it behind her.

His buddies have been watching from the bar, and now they cluster around him. "Hey Arnie, what happened?"

"I've no idea. Everything was going great. Chicks! Who can understand them?"

Memories: Early, Early

A WOMAN SOMETIMES REMEMBERS before she was born. Not the womb-time, but back farther, farther: her mother a child, her father also, and she was already dreaming herself inside them, though they couldn't know that yet, or could they? Them not knowing about her exactly, but knowing something. Twists and turns curling ahead of them like DNA strands, so they couldn't see into the future, even though their minds were always searching, peering like flashlights into the gloom.

The woman remembers things like that, but not what she had for breakfast. Anyway, what does it matter? What to cook for supper is more important, trying to imagine a meal, and shop for ingredients ahead of time.

Looking backward seems so much easier.

Snapshots: that little mother, a child in white ruffles; that small father in knee pants and long socks. Them growing this way and that, almost aimless, but someone planning it ahead. Her, unborn, directing her parents as best she could. Future generations were coiled inside them, like lists of begats inside a Bible.

That little old-fashioned girl who would someday be her Momma: there she is, sitting on her father's knee, following her own mother around the kitchen, trying to copy and be just like her, except prettier and younger, so her father would like her best.

That little boy who would be her Papa, following his mother wherever she went, imprinting on her sweet quiet gentleness.

And herself, already coiled in the darkness inside them, watching, instinctive, knowing more than she does today.

Her memories keep flipping backward, like riffled pages in an album; some of the pictures falling out, getting ripped. Her parents fading into shadows while she grabs at them, frantic, trying to fasten them back together before they disappear, are lost forever.

Sometimes their memories flicker like fireflies inside her mind, or shimmer like candlelight on shiny tile. Ancient mist swirls around her. She lolls in a bathtub of perfumed oils, floating backward to that womb the whole world emerged from. Unborn creatures drift around her, their big eyes peering through a blur of fluid, thin tissue of amniotic sac, while the pregnant earth keeps moving, throbbing, *lub dub, lub dub.*

And now a new birth is about to happen. She thinks she is almost ready. She has a cradle and flannelette blankets; she has diapers and booties and little gowns with fake smocking. She has decided on two names: Robert for a boy, and Roberta for a girl.

But then the pains begin, and keep coming. They never stop. She has never imagined this much terrible pain. She sends her husband away. She doesn't want him near her; that's how this pain got started in the first place.

Surely she will be able to stand it; somehow other women do. It helps that she believes the pain will stop once she is able to push the child out of her body. She is only eighteen-years-old and doesn't realize that children cause their parents grief throughout their lives. Anyway, it's fair. The parents cause their children sorrow, too.

She couldn't make Momma happy, but that wasn't her fault. Or was it? Was it? No, of course not. But anyway she is certain her own child will bring only perfect bliss.

The woman sometimes remembers before she was born.

She never tells anyone about this. Well, of course not. They'd think she was crazy.

Missed Carriage

MISCARRIAGE IS WHAT MOMMA SAYS, but missed carriage is what Debbie hears. Momma is going to have a baby, and Debbie will get a little brother or sister to play with, but it doesn't happen because of a missed carriage.

Poor little ghost baby with no carriage to ride inside. And where is that baby now? Not in their part of the graveyard where the names of dead relatives are printed on slabs of cement, with the dates when they were born and when they died. Debbie can add and subtract by now, so she knows there aren't any babies there. It hasn't a carriage and isn't old enough to walk, so where could that poor little baby have gone? Then Debbie sees a Bible painting of cherub babies sitting on clouds, and realizes ghost babies must be able to fly like pigeons.

The bird-lady in the next apartment keeps a canary singing in a cage. Sometimes she wears binoculars around her neck, and wanders along the beach, writing down bird names in a little notebook. Debbie asks if one of the birds was a ghost-baby, but the woman doesn't understand. Apparently she's not a very good bird-lady after all.

These days Momma is lying in bed when Debbie leaves for school, and still there when she comes home. Soon Grandma starts coming over to cook their meals, so Momma never bothers to get up at all. "Taking it easy" is what Momma calls it, and this time Debbie finally gets a baby sister. But the baby is not much good. It just lies there; it can't play games.

Baby Sally drinks milk that squirts out of Momma's nipples. "Did you feed me like that?" Debbie asks, but when Momma says yes, Debbie throws up in the toilet and never watches Momma feeding nipple-milk again.

The baby cries a lot, and Momma pushes the carriage back and forth, back and forth while she sings lullaby-songs, the same ones over and over.

"Momma? Did you ever sing those songs to me?" Suddenly it is important for Debbie to know this.

"No, dear. I didn't need to. You never cried."

"I didn't know I was supposed to." But Debbie mutters this under her breath. She knows there's no point saying it aloud.

The baby has a name, but Papa calls it "our little Christmas bonus." He laughs and tells their friends, "We finally learned what to do," and the men laugh too loud, and the women's laughs squeak higher and higher until the sound hurts Debbie's ears.

Everyone is happy about this Christmas-bonus baby. Except Papa who has to work harder to make enough money. Except Momma who is tired all day long. Except Debbie who has to be Momma's little helper. "Whatever would I do without you?" Momma says this all the time, when she asks Debbie to run to the store for groceries, or push the carriage back and forth and sing songs to the Christmas-bonus baby.

Now there isn't enough space in the apartment, so the family moves into a house. Bungalow, her parents call it; Debbie says it backwards: a low bunga. Either way it is true; their house is lower than the neighbours' houses. Debbie's best friend lives next door and walks upstairs to go to bed, and can climb up even higher into an attic where she and Debbie are allowed to play. They dress up in old clothes and pretend to be fairy princesses or Cinderella or Snow White. Sometimes they are brave and turn off the light to play hide and seek in the dark.

This is what life is like when Debbie is eleven years old and they all live together in their low bunga: Momma and Papa and their sweet children.

Then one more surprise happens: Papa packs up his clothes and moves away. Momma takes Debbie and the baby to spend that day at the beach, where Momma stares at the waves, and the baby gets a sunburn, and Debbie builds lovely sand castles with turrets and flag-poles and moats. Finally they get thirsty and grouchy and go back home.

Debbie can't find Papa anywhere, and thinks he must be playing a game of hide-and-seek, so she searches inside closets and under beds but can't find him anywhere. The baby is crying for her milk, but Momma ignores her and goes to bed with a bad headache. Debbie keeps searching, pulling open his empty bureau drawers, looking for clues, while the baby finally cries itself to sleep.

The car is gone, too, but it doesn't matter; Momma never learned how to drive.

A Moving Story

AMANDA AND THE DOG GROW UP together. There's a photo on Holly's dresser: Amanda and Skippy sitting inside the playpen watching for the flash. The cat came later.

Amanda keeps growing older. "Tell me a story," she begs, trying to put off bedtime. Holly can never refuse. The child feels so fragile, her arms and legs long and spindly. Holly runs her fingers up and down Amanda's back, counting the nubbins of spine, counting ribs.

"Okay. Now pay attention. This is about the time when you were a bird."

"Really? I used to be a bird?"

"I never said the story was true. Hush now. Just listen. The world was young then, and an egg lay deep in a nest hidden up high in the branches of a sugar maple tree..."

"No, Mummy. I want a story that really happened. Tell about the day we moved."

Holly loves a chance to talk about it again. Remembering her exhaustion from all the packing and unpacking boxes helps control her restlessness.

"Okay. This is the story of coming to this place, but all moves are pretty much the same. Moving day always starts out sunny. The rain or snow or sleet never starts until it's time to unload the truck. It's a law. Like the one that says moving takes twice as long as you had expected.

"So there we were, moving again, and this time you were big enough to help. Not like last year when you were only three years old and got in everyone's way. That was fun, too, though. Can you remember?"

Amanda shakes her head and looks confused.

"Never mind. I'll just tell about this time. After everything was in the truck, Uncle Ronny put you up on his shoulders and carried you around the old apartment. He made up a moving song and you both shouted it out as loud as you could. '*Goodbye ceiling, goodbye floor. Goodbye window, goodbye door.*' It was such a great song."

"That's right," Amanda remembers. "And we sang a hello song to this place when we got here."

Holly and Amanda sing it now, wandering around the apartment, their fingers reaching up toward the ceiling, but able to touch everything else: "*Hello ceiling, hello floor. Hello window, hello door.*" Over and over.

Holly gets bored first and wants some new verses, so Amanda thinks some up. "*Hello sink, hello tub...*"

"*That the old tenants never bothered to scrub.*"

"*Hello top floor of the house...*"

"*Hello cockroach. Hello mouse.*"

"*Hello barking downstairs dog...*"

Log. Cog. Fog. The ugly landlord grunts like a hog. Holly's not going to tell Amanda that, but now the words thump back and forth inside her head so she can't think of a different line. "Never mind. Maybe we should leave the song alone. It's already perfect."

"Anyway," she continues, "there we were, moving again. We hadn't bought anything new since the last time, but the move took longer, anyway. Maybe because everyone who helped was one year older and one year slower. Or maybe the world around us had sped up in the meantime.

"You helped me measure everything ahead of time. That's how we knew the rug would cover the floor vent unless we rolled up one end and hid it behind the couch, and it's how we were sure the drapes wouldn't fit. Drapes never fit a new place, anyway. They are always too short or too narrow. Never too big. That's another moving day law."

Amanda has fallen asleep, but Holly keeps remembering.

Moving day. The day Holly discovered the previous tenant had skipped out owing six weeks of newspaper delivery.

Moving day. Ronny brought along the kitty litter complete with cat poop, but forgot the cat and had to go back.

Someone stacked a carton labelled BOOKS on top of another labelled FRAGILE.

On moving night, Holly and Amanda went to bed with unbrushed teeth. This always happens. The toothpaste and brushes had been safely packed inside a carton labelled MIS-CELLANEOUS, but that word was on most of the cartons.

The trouble with packing is forgetting that boxes might not be unpacked for years. Holly always moves to some place smaller, but takes everything she owns just in case there's enough room. There never is. Unpacked boxes get stacked up and covered with pieces of fabric so she can pretend they are really tables.

Let's have a yoga move next time, she thinks. Let's sit cross-legged on the floor and meditate to somewhere else. Let's have a zen move. Let's imagine we've moved already, and just stay put.

Let's have a humane society move and give the cat and dog away. Let's have an orphan move and give away the kid. "Just kidding," she reassures Amanda, who's still asleep.

Let's give away our friends so we don't have to send change-of-address cards.

Let's drag all our belongings outside and try to sell them. Anything that's left over we'll give away.

Let's move with just one suitcase. Let it be empty. We'll carry that empty suitcase anyway, so the world will know we're moving on.

Not that she plans to move again. Not right away. She likes this place. But she will move. Of course. Other people need roots, but Holly needs an absence of them. No ties. None. Except for Amanda; except for the dog and cat.

Moving every year is some kind of a tradition, and kids need rituals, Holly tells herself, patterns they can count on. She imagines Amanda, all grown-up, telling bedtime stories to a little daughter of her own, describing her childhood, telling about moving every year. Amanda's stories will keep getting richer, more ridiculous, as she drags in all her old memories, embellishing, adding fantastic new adventures, describing her restless mother who became claustrophobic whenever it was time to renew a lease. "She would rip it up into little pieces and stuff them in an envelope labelled, ONE YEAR IS MORE THAN ENOUGH!, then shove it through the landlord's mail slot."

Will Amanda describe her mother as a sweet eccentric or as just plain weird? Holly will have to be there to defend herself, to make sure Amanda gets all the details right.

But she won't be. Of course not. That's what moving on is all about. Amanda will leave her childhood behind, including her mother. Discarding, like Holly did; like she still does.

She glances at her watch, eight thirty in the evening, and wonders what her mother is doing back in Toronto. Probably nothing. Putting in time. How can she stand it? Sipping a cup of tea with the old battle-axe in the next apartment, playing euchre at the community centre, watching the soaps on TV, staring at the telephone, thinking she might as well disconnect it because Holly never bothers to call.

Dammit, Holly thinks. It's the way of the world: you spend a couple of decades, the best years of your life, raising your kids so they can turn into adults who move away and never look back.

But dammit, Momma has her friends and lots of memories. Surely that should be enough. But of course it isn't. Okay, then. Maybe next year's move should be to Toronto. Children need grandparents to spoil them, and probably the reverse is also true: grandmas need youngsters to spoil.

Anyway, if she stays in Halifax, sooner or later she might run into her old boyfriend. It's too late now for him to meet Amanda, to do the math, and realize he must be the father.

Amanda stirs. "Hey, I fell asleep. Tell me some more."

"Okay, but pay attention. This is important."

Neighbours

A MAN IS IN THE NEXT-DOOR GARDEN. He is digging a hole. I watch from my window, fascinated, although I hate him. I watch and wonder what he is doing.

At first he is only visible above the knees, then above the hips, the chest, the neck. He disappears, but I can see his arms raising the shovel. Then only the shovel. Then only the dirt, which bursts into the air at regular intervals like a pulse beat, like the spurt of blood from a cut artery, or the spouting of a geyser from some mysterious underground source.

He clambers out from time to time and shovels the pile of dirt back from the edge. Then he lies down on his stomach on the ground and peers into the hole he has made. Soon he disappears over the edge again, taking his shovel.

It is a long time since he last climbed out.

Perhaps he is in trouble, having chest pains or a stroke. Perhaps the shovel slipped and sliced his foot, blood slowly moistening the soil around him. Maybe he is still bleeding, becoming pale and paler, turning as white as all creatures who live far beneath the surface of the earth.

It is dark now. I can see nothing, but I know he is down there.

Probably there is something I should do, call the police for instance, but surely he has not broken any law.

A ladder lies on his lawn. He may have intended to take it with him. It would have been awkward for him to dig, with the bottom of the ladder always in the way of the shovel. He would wait until it became difficult to climb out before placing the ladder inside the hole.

Perhaps he forgot to do this, until he was no longer able to reach it. What would he do then? Call out? Keep on digging? Sit down and cry?

He knows I am the only person who could hear him. No one lives near us. He knows I would not answer because I hate him.

I can imagine the things he would tell me if I went out there, if I lay down on my stomach at the edge where I could listen. "Forgive me," he would plead. "I never meant to turn everyone against you with my stories. I believed the stories when I told them, but I don't any longer. They are lies. When I get out I will tell everyone I made them up. They will all turn against me and welcome you with open arms."

"We will become friends," he would continue, "and live next door to each other in perfect peace. We will grow old, and laugh about past differences.

"We will do this, unless you prefer I move away. If you want me to I'll be gone by morning. I'll leave a note on my front door explaining that I left of my own free will and won't be back. I have a cousin in South America who needs my help."

Perhaps this is the sort of thing he would tell me if I would listen.

I might throw a bit of earth down the hole. I would do this for a joke, just to scare him. To let him see that I have power. To make him beg.

I might do this a few times, just to get even, before I put the ladder down the hole to let him out.

He is trapped. He is deeper than earthworms and slugs, deeper than small animals that burrow into the ground for safety. He is beyond them.

The creatures he visits now have never been disturbed. They have never seen light, but their bodies contain remnants of light sensors and optic nerves, left over from ancient times. Long ago their ancestors climbed out of shallow holes each night to feed; these descendants live far deeper in the earth and never rise to the surface at all, surviving by metabolizing dirt. No one has ever seen them, but scientists believe in their existence, detecting a slight motion with their powerful seismographic probes.

These animals must hate him as I do. He has disturbed them with his digging. Right now, even at night, the faint decrease in blackness must cause them pain. In the morning light they will begin screaming. They will continue to scream until someone fills up the hole. Perhaps even then they will scream, but no one will have to listen.

They are innocent. They never asked to have this happen. I could help them. I have a shovel.

Newspaper Report

"OMIGOD!" SAYS MERLE, rattling the newspaper. She has Danny's attention. "Yeah? What?"

"Just a sec." So he waits while Merle keeps reading. Then, "Geez Danny, what's the craziest way to commit suicide you've ever heard of?"

Danny just waits for Merle to tell him.

"C'mon Danny. What's the stupidest? Just give it a try, but you'll never get it."

No way Danny's going to waste his time trying to answer. Merle always asks dumb questions like that. "What's the scariest dream you ever had?" "Your best memory?" "Your worst one?" "Your favourite movie star?" "Favourite colour?" It drives him crazy. "If you found a genie in a bottle what three things would you ask for?" "If you could go anywhere in the world where would it be?" "If you won the bonanza at bingo...." Danny can't stand it.

Merle sees things so simplistically. It reminds him of his grade four teacher: Write a composition on *My Favourite Person, My Nicest Day, The Best Summer Holiday I Ever Had.*

"Give up?" Merle asks. "You might as well. You'll never get it. Honestly, this is so gross. This woman in the newspaper, she wanted to commit suicide, so she injected someone's blood into her arm. The blood was from a dying person! My God! Isn't that sick!"

Danny doesn't believe her. "Lemme see." He grabs the paper

but Merle is still holding on tight so the article rips right up the middle.

"Now see what you've done!" Merle hollers. "I try to tell you something from the newspaper and you go and spoil it."

"Lemme see that. You must have got it wrong."

They hold the paper together and try to read it. "Stop jiggling," he says. "Stop jiggling yourself," Merle answers back, and so on.

It's right there in black and white. Some woman wanted to commit suicide and had a friend dying from some weird tropical disease. Maybe he was her lover and she wanted to kill herself because he was dying. The paper doesn't give any details. She injected herself with some of his blood, but then later…

"…Later she changed her mind," Danny reads aloud. "Jesus!" he yells, "I guess so! Like when she noticed what she had done. When she popped back to her senses. When she woke up."

"The poor woman," says Merle.

They think about her, dying slowly, for however long it takes. "About a year," says Danny. "It would probably take a year." Merle disagrees. "More than that. Five years maybe." They argue back and forth a little bit but their hearts aren't in it.

"Maybe they'll be able to cure it," Danny suggests, ever hopeful, but Merle says he just doesn't want to face facts.

Meanwhile, somewhere in the world a woman regrets and regrets that bad decision. She is pale and thin; her bones stick out. Her knees are bruised from kneeling on the floor beside her bed. "I was out of my mind," she explains. "You must have known, God. You could see I was acting crazy. It wasn't my fault. C'mon, God. Just make it better. Just this one favour. I promise I'll never ask for anything else."

All over North America people read their evening papers. They find out about this woman and feel sick. They say to one another, "This is it. This is the ultimate. I'm not going to read newspapers anymore. There's no point. Nothing can top this," and they never buy newspapers again.

A lot of jobs are lost of course: journalists, editors, delivery truck drivers.... But ex-readers don't care. They start feeling good about trees not being chopped down for pulpwood. Maybe they daydream of jack pines somewhere up north, reaching higher and higher inside the sky, their branches soaking up fresh air and sunshine.

If that woman is still out there dying of some weird disease, they don't want to know.

After the soaps they click off their TV sets to avoid the news. They intend to switch them on later to watch a favourite sit-com, but they're already involved in something else and have forgotten. Families play monopoly or scrabble, fit jigsaw puzzles together, collect coins and stamps, polish rocks. They bake muffins and chocolate chip cookies. Parents fasten snapshots in albums and tell stories about the old days. Kids spend more time on homework and start getting better grades. Folks stock up on library books. They go to bed early. Couples aren't too tired to touch each other. Love happens, and sometimes babies get started.

Ratings plummet. TV stores go out of business. Talk show hosts apply for unemployment insurance, and later, welfare.

Wars stop happening. Politicians can't be bothered bickering because their constituents won't know about it. All the news that used to be reported gradually stops taking place: rapes, robberies, murders. Streets become safe. No one mugs old ladies or anyone else.

People relax, read to their children. They take walks, plant gardens, chat with neighbours, loll on porch gliders that swing gently to and fro.

An extra person dies. It's a small price to pay. But not for that woman, of course.

Paper Serviettes

JERRY IS WATCHING A WOMAN two tables away. She is gazing out the window, but seems awkward and self-conscious, as though trying to give the impression that her mind is a million miles away. Every once in a while she doodles on a paper serviette. Once he had a wife who did that, scrawled little images on scraps of paper, envelopes, whatever was handy, even the wall, her knee, her arm, while her phone conversations never missed a beat: "Yeah? What happened then? Did he speak to you or not? What'd he say?" She always doodled the same old trees and flowers: barren winter trees, with sunflowers stretching up to reach the empty branches. She never bothered to sketch anything else, and didn't care about the seasonal anachronism no matter how often he pointed it out. He can hardly remember what his wife looked like, but he can still see those stupid scribbles.

Jerry hates remembering his ex-wife, so he focuses on the coffee-shop woman instead. It's going to be hard to describe her in a way that makes her distinctive: mousey hair, middling age, average this, ordinary that.

Whoops, she's staring at him. Has he looked at her way too often? Has she misunderstood his attention? Maybe. So he looks elsewhere, stares at traffic beyond the window; that way, his glance will seem merely haphazard. He glances her way later and sees that she is staring at him again. Maybe she never stopped. This is embarrassing. Is she waiting for him to approach her, to say something? She'll just have to wait, then, wait on and on, and eventually be disappointed. Too bad for her. Tough luck.

Still, it's kind of flattering to be stared at. To be found interesting, maybe even attractive. He straightens his shoulders, pulls in his gut, runs his fingers through what's left of his hair.

He begins to create a story around her, but it isn't easy. She's too ordinary.

The guy at the next table looks like a guy she used to know, a boy she had a high school crush on. She has been searching for him ever since, in one donut shop after another. Tonight she thought at last she'd found him, but on closer inspection it turned out to be someone else after all. She ought to hire a private detective but can't afford one. Besides, if she really found that guy from high school, what would she do? Speak up? Of course not. She's too shy. She'd rather daydream than take action. She's such a nothing, a nebbish; ought to take assertiveness courses, develop some backbone....

Or,

The woman gave up an infant for adoption fifteen years ago and has regretted it ever since. She studies teenage girls, watching for some family resemblance. Worrying what would she do if she found one who looked like snapshots of herself when she was in her teens? She should have been brave and kept that baby, despite the preacher, despite her parents with their rigid small-town morality, and the whispers of gossiping old women with nothing better to do. She should have clutched her baby tight, moved to the city, and gone on welfare while she learned some marketable skill. She could have managed, but had no idea, at seventeen, how strong she would eventually become....

Or,

An abandoned wife. The husband knew right away he'd made a mistake. She isn't the kind of woman he's usually attracted to. Sweet though, and affectionate, kind of reminding him of a spaniel. The kind of woman he could take home to his mother: "Look, Ma. See who I've married. She'll fit right into the family. And you kept saying I'd never settle down." But he had never wanted the kind of woman his folks would approve of. He'd thought she was different, but no. He tried having other women on the side but that just made him more discontented. He'd come home after working late at the office and find her hair already in pin curls, bobby pins bristling from her head like a porcupine....

Oops. Not pin curls. They're too old-fashioned. Foam rollers, maybe. Anyway, he can check out hair routines later. Right now the words are flowing and he'd better keep writing. But if ever he saw a woman who'd use pin curls, she's the one. If she ever combs her hair at all....

She ought to throw that ponytail elastic in the garbage and get her hair trimmed. Maybe have a rinse to give her highlights. But she doesn't have much money, not enough for make-up either. Just a dab of pale lipstick, nothing else. That's what happens when you're raised religious. But she worries about getting wrinkles, so slathers on cold cream every night to prevent them. That poor husband. No wonder he doesn't come home. He can't stand the smell of that cream. It reminds him of his mother. He tries coming home later and later to avoid her, but she's patient and forgiving and waits up anyway. Pedestrians glance at her window and think they've seen a ghost, her pale face even whiter from its coating of cold cream....

Or,

She has just learned she has cancer and can't bear being alone in her tiny third floor flat. Even TV sitcoms cannot distract her. She needs real people around her, so she can feel sympathetic toward them, because for all she knows their problems may be even greater than hers. But of course not. Nothing is worse than cancer. Tonight she needs people, in all their wild variety; the weirder the better. Winos, bag ladies, teenage hoodlums, welfare bums.... She needs voices, a radio in the background playing sad western music, the glare of fluorescent lights. A chocolate donut with chocolate icing. No, make that two. What the heck, why not? What difference can it make? Plus a large coffee, double double. Maybe she'll buy a pack of cigarettes and start smoking again, because the cancer's not in her lungs. Close, though. A bit of dimpling by the left nipple. The doctor found it at her annual check-up. If she hadn't kept that appointment she wouldn't even know. Though she might have found the lump herself, if she had ever bothered to check them. Maybe her lover would have noticed, if she'd had one....

What would it mean to a woman to lose a breast? Would it be like a guy having a testicle removed? He can't imagine, has no idea. Anyway, he can't imagine losing a testicle either.

Probably no one has ever sucked her breasts; not a lover, not an infant, so she won't know what she'll be missing. Anyway, she'll still have one breast left. Or no. The other one went first, nearly five years ago. She'd been keeping track of the time and thought she was finally safe....

She's standing up, heading to the washroom. Is she limping a bit? Maybe from childhood polio. She missed getting the vaccine. How come? Perhaps her parents belonged to some extremist religious sect. He'll need to find out which one objects to vaccination. But there's no rush. Right now the muse is co-operating, his mind is hot, as he tries to imagine what her hospital stay would have been like.

In her early teens, immobile, trapped inside a respirator, an iron lung, afraid she would never walk or skip or dance again. But she had managed. She had persevered with all those exercises: in the therapeutic pool at first, then later in the physio department. She had proved all those pessimists wrong....

Linda's leg is stiff from sitting too long. She licks cinnamon sugar from her fingers, tucks some paper serviettes into her pocket. Then she gathers up her coloured pens: green for short stories, pink for poetry, blue for everything else. Betsy will still be sound asleep, and Frank sprawled on the sofa, a clutter of empty beer bottles at his feet, probably in a bad mood from watching the Leafs lose again. If she comes in the side door and he doesn't notice, perhaps she can copy her notes into her journal while they're still fresh.

A man chews sugarless gum. He has gum disease now and worries about his breath. How can he possibly know how it smells to other people? Especially women. At the office he cups his hand in front of his face whenever he has to talk to people, especially women, but he's afraid they notice this and laugh behind his back. He is right. They also laugh at how he combs a few strands of long hair sideways, trying to cover up his bald spot. He hopes no one notices this, but of course everyone does. Anyway, as if women mind baldness anymore. Not since Yul Brynner and Telly Salvalas. But they laugh at guys who comb their hair this way. The woman he lives with should tell him, but she doesn't. She laughs too....

The woman has gone now. He might as well leave, too. As he struggles into his jacket, he stares out the window at buses and cars. Lots of people, all travelling somewhere. He tries to remember what that was like.

The waitress sighs. "Finally. I thought they'd never leave." She refills the serviette containers on both tables. "Damn writers. We should charge them extra."

Postcards

ALISON NEVER MEANT TO BE the one who stayed in Toronto. She intended to leave the city far behind, and travel to places that sounded exotic: Cuba, Australia, the Galapagos Islands, Madagascar.... She would mail folks postcards of exotic scenery and decorate the cards with foreign postage stamps; everyone would be jealous. Instead, she got pregnant in high school and she and Buddy had to get married. Then she spent years taking care of other people: raising her own sweet children, bringing meals to Momma. But Momma is dead now, the girls have grown up, and her husband moved out a couple of months ago. Now Alison is able to change her ordinary life, but can't figure out how. She is forty-five years old already (how can this have happened?) and it feels too late, way too late.

All the same, lately she has been receiving postcards from herself. Each morning she finds another on the bedside table. She recognizes the handwriting of course, though she hasn't written in that rounded script since her teens. Sometimes they start out, "Hi!" without adding a name. Well, of course not. Alison already knows who she is, so writing her name would be redundant. Usually there's no salutation at all, as though the writer is simply continuing a conversation.

I need money to buy some clothes I like, instead of the sappy ones Momma sews from remnants. I finally found a Saturday job at Simpson's selling children's shoes. It turns out that babies have square fat feet and scrunch them up. It's hard to shove their feet into lace-up baby boots, squishing this little piggy, squishing that one. The parents try to help. The little babies yell because it hurts, and I want to yell right back: "Hey, do you think I like to do this? I hate it. It's just a job." But I guess torturers always say this. Poor little babies being tormented like Jesus on a cross or Joan of Arc burned at the stake. A cute boy works in my department. I don't know his name yet. Sometimes we talk in the stock room. It takes a long time to find the right size shoes.

In these postcards Alison is always a teenager, and this seems to make sense, because lately she seems to have turned into one again. Maybe this time she won't bother to grow up and pretend to be an adult; she might just dwell in that world of high school angst forever. It's Buddy's fault. Isn't everything? If only he had gone to a different high school.

So, I bought some jersey material and got Momma to stitch me up a pink sack dress for dancing. It's real easy. Probably I could have done it myself. Just sew straight up the sides and along the top, but leave three holes for the arms and neck. Everyone wears them. They just hang there and look enormous until we gather them in with something. A cinch belt is the best, but they cost money so I use an old tie of Papa's. All us girls wear different pastel colours and we look like a flower garden, but when I say so they look at me like I'm crazy, so I pretend I'm just kidding. But at church dances we ARE like a row of flowers, nodding curly blossom heads as we talk, waiting for some boy to come by and pluck. Like ripping petals off daisies. She loves me, she loves me not. That word "wallflower," I bet that's where it comes from.

Every day another missive from her past.

I got transferred to chocolates for Christmas. Vanilla creams are my favourite, also anything with nuts. Toffees take too long to chew. I can't decide which I like best, light chocolate or dark. The ancient fossil-lady in charge must have sold candies forever. I watch but she never sneaks one. Maybe she's sick of them by now after eighty or a hundred years. Probably they made all her teeth fall out. But I'm just here for the Christmas holidays so this is the only chance I've got. Customers point at which ones they want and I put them in cute little crinkly paper cups. Sometimes people take forever to decide, so I tell them my favourites to hurry them up. Buddy is teaching me the names of cars now. He knows which year is which. We sit on the curb and watch them. So far I know Pontiac and Ford and Chevy.

Alison tosses the cards in a bureau drawer. There are lots of empty ones to choose from.

We go to dances Friday nights. United Church or Holy Mary. Catholic churches have names that sound like swearing: Holy Peter, Holy Jesus. All us girls stand around together and yak as fast as we can. We act so cool, like we don't care if someone asks us to dance or not. Like, do they think we came here just for dancing? Maybe we'd rather just yak with our girlfriends. Don't the boys ever think about that? Or maybe a Hollywood producer notices and thinks we'd be perfect in the movies, like The Flying Nun or Gidget. The music starts, so we go to the ladies room to fix our lipstick and don't come out till the music stops. I don't care about dancing, anyway. I just want some guy to walk me home. Then Buddy will see him and be jealous and invite me out next weekend. That's the plan.

The queen-size bed seems enormous. Alison heaps the clean laundry on one side. Perhaps eventually she'll fold it. For now it simply fills up that empty space. Good.

I hate house parties the worst. Always one girl is blonde and pretty and laughs a lot and all the boys are paying attention. She goes in the bedroom with a boy so they can do whatever they want and we can't watch. The rest of us pretend we don't notice. We eat potato chips and yak about whatever's happening at school these days. We might as well have brought our homework and be doing it right now. Her hair needs combing after. It doesn't matter, though. Boys don't care about rumpled clothes or tangled hair. I don't want to go in that bedroom, but I want some boy to ask me.

Books and magazines are piled on the bed so Alison can read herself to sleep. She wakes up a couple of hours later, the overhead light on, her glasses askew, her teeth unbrushed and feeling scummy; then she reads herself to sleep again, wakes up later, and so on. "Sleeping okay?" her friends keep asking, and she always answers, "Yeah. Of course. Why not?"

I got switched to Viewmasters. You put a cardboard circle in a little machine and hold it up to the light, then click, click, to get another picture. The colours are bright and fake like Mickey Mouse cartoons. I don't ever want to travel to foreign countries as bright and shiny as that. Trees and mountains jump right at you, like watching a 3-D movie. It's really weird, but I'm learning to be polite: "Yes ma'am, this thing's real easy. Educational, too. Your little kid will love it. You'll need some more reels for him to look at. How about lions and tigers? Maybe sharks or spiders or snakes? It's okay. Little kids like scary stuff."

Rita wants to meet for supper or a movie. Marsha wants to meet in a coffee shop and yak. "No." "No thank you." "No." A neighbour's bridge club needs someone to sub because some old lady had a stroke or broke a hip. Maisie has found a perfect guy for Alison to meet. "Sorry. I'm busy. Can't talk now. I'll call back later."

The typewriter keys at school are black instead of letters. There's a chart to look at instead. We're supposed to know where each finger is. I never know. How come they pay that teacher? She just stands there with a stop-watch and calls out when time is up. Then we pass our pages to someone else to mark. I always make the most mistakes. Why can't we learn something useful instead? Woodworking maybe? Momma drives me crazy these days and I drive her bats right back. Nothing I do is right. She hates jeans, also T-shirts, even though mine don't have any messages. She just likes sappy clothes like she wore when she was my age. I've seen those old snapshots and tell her, "No way. I'd rather have friends." She doesn't like my friends either. Well, neither do I. Girls are so boring these days. All they talk about is boys.

Alison doesn't bother returning calls. People are starting to sound hurt or angry. "Alison, I know you're there. It's me. Pick up the phone."

Buddy and me go to lots of house parties these days. Diana went to a funeral in the afternoon and a party the same night. That's so rude. She should have stayed home. Anyway, she told us what a funeral is like. The dead person was her grandma. Diana was scared to touch her. Probably she cried. I don't ever want to know anyone who dies. The teachers keep giving us too much homework, algebra equations, useless things like that. We waste all day in school. Isn't that enough? They shouldn't expect us to do more at night? I've got to write a stupid essay: Three Causes of the Industrial Revolution. The war of 1812 was just the same. How come there's always exactly three causes of everything? School is boring except for boys.

Christmas is coming. The geese are getting fat and so is Alison. She keeps a tin of cookies on top of her bedside table and chocolate bars hidden inside the drawer. In the middle of the night candy wrappers crunch beneath her pillow and wake her up. She sips at a can of pop because chocolate always makes her thirsty. Or perhaps she's fat because of being pregnant. She wonders a lot about that. She and Buddy had sex not too long before he left. Maybe the week before? When was that exactly? She can't remember.

Everyone always asks what I'll be when I grow up. Teachers and neighbours, aunts and uncles. It's none of their business. I tell them I just want to hurry up and be a grown-up so folks will stop asking snoopy questions. Buddy knows a new way to kiss me now. He puts his tongue inside my mouth and expects me to like it. Yuck. It's disgusting, but I pretend it's really great. But now I'm scared. Can this get me pregnant? I can't ask anyone this question. They'll think I'm stupid.

Alison thinks about abortion. She thinks about raising another child, this time on her own. Other women do it; she could, too. She would have to move away though, so Buddy wouldn't find out and try to weasel his way into its life. But their daughters would be sure to tell him. And what if the baby looked just like him? Could she stand it?

I hate English except for "The Ballad of Reading Gaol."[1] G-A-O-L. That means jail, the way they spell it wrong in England. Also, "The Bridge of Sighs."[2] But it's so sad. A woman drowns in a river. I think maybe it's suicide, but I'm not absolutely sure. Probably I'll flunk out of school anyway, because of failing gym class. I can't turn a backward somersault or stand on my head. And forget about ever getting over top of that vault box. It's way too high. The other kids ask if I'm scared. Are they stupid? Of course I am. They should be, too. What if I fell and broke my neck? I'd be in a wheelchair or hospital bed forever. We wear ugly romper gym suits and have to get changed in the wide-open locker room. Everyone watches everyone else, checking out boobs and bums.

Forty-five years old. Isn't that too old to get pregnant? Alison isn't sure. Maybe this is menopause. Anyway, her periods are always irregular and she never knows when to expect them.

Momma yells at me all the time and I yell right back. I need black ballerina shoes for dances but she buys some other kind on sale and can't return them. I yell at her to keep them for herself. She's so old. It doesn't matter what kind of clothes she wears. I wish I knew Spanish or Latin or any language she can't understand. I could swear and call her names whenever I want. Probably that's how pig latin got started.

Alison worries that she's too old to have a healthy baby. The fetus might be defective, whatever that means. Toes or fingers missing. A leaky heart valve. A locked door inside the spinal cord or brain.

> The neighbours always ask me to babysit. I don't want to but can never think of a good excuse. They always promise the baby will stay asleep but it never does. It starts crying the minute they leave, and I feel like crying, too. The baby's too small to sit on a toilet so it poops in its pants instead. It's so disgusting. The baby wriggles around while I change it and I'm scared of poking it with a diaper pin. Another thing, how am I supposed to know whether the bottle of milk is warm enough? Do the parents expect me to taste it myself? Yuck! But I'm scared of burning a tiny stomach so I give it milk straight from the fridge. That way I know it's safe. I'm never going to get married unless the guy swears he never wants kids.

Defective. She should be worrying about that, but doesn't really care. Because she would love the baby, anyway. She knows that much. Anyway, it's not like the old days. Employers hire people with disabilities now. They have to. There's probably a quota. A man in a wheelchair works in the mailroom at the mall. A woman with Down's Syndrome clears away the cafeteria trays.

> Buddy kisses me that way all the time now. He says it's French. Those people in France are disgusting. I'm still scared it might make me pregnant. I keep waiting for my period but I don't keep track of the dates so never know when it should come.

One morning the sheets are stained with blood. Finally. At

last. Alison is relieved of course, but also disappointed because it had been her last chance. She'll never have another baby now. She would have to find a new partner first. She'd have to want one.

> The school nurse owns all the aspirins. You need a headache to get to see her. She says French kissing can't get you pregnant and acts like it's a stupid question. She wants to tell more stuff about sex, but I say my headache's okay now and walk out. It's none of her business.

Alison wakes up feeling rested. She checks her bedside table: no postcards. Somehow, she's not surprised. It is Saturday, the sun is shining and the city is waiting to be explored. She could start with the farmer's market. While she sips her morning coffee, she picks up the telephone and begins returning calls: Rita, Marsha, Annie... They don't answer, so Alison leaves messages on their machines.

---

[1] Oscar Wilde. *The Ballad of Reading Gaol* (Leonard Smithers, 1898).
[2] Thomas Hood. "The Bridge of Sighs." *Shorter Poems* (1924).

Smile. You're on a Greyhound Bus

ELLEN IS ON THE ROAD AGAIN, needing to leave Toronto, trying to imagine life in each small town she passes through. Each one presents a new possibility. Sooner or later she will have to decide, gather her belongings, disembark, begin a new life.

She becomes aware of voices behind her, a young woman, an older man. She doesn't want to hear this conversation, and wonders what she should do.

"I like your smile."

Silence.

"Do you mind me sitting here?"

"No. Free country."

"Would you rather sit by yourself?"

"No. It's okay."

"Thanks. I like sitting beside you. I like it a lot. Where are you going?"

Silence.

"What's your name?"

"Katie."

"Katie. That's a nice name."

"Thanks."

"I want to be your friend."

Silence

"I'm forty-one years old. A bit older than you. How old are you anyway?"

"Sixteen."

"Sixteen? Really?"

Silence.

Only sixteen. A teenager who needs protection. Ellen can't ignore the conversation any longer. She turns around, glares at the man. "Listen, you creep, leave this youngster alone. Move to a different seat or I'll report you to the driver."

But the girl is the one who answers back. "Shut up, you old hag. Mind your own business. I've already got one mother. She's more than enough."

So Ellen tries to ignore their conversation, but they seem to be talking louder, probably trying to provoke her. If so, it works.

"I want to be your friend. Do you know what a friend is?"

"Yes."

"That's good then."

Silence.

"Do you have a boyfriend? It's all right. You can tell me."

"Yes."

"You do? Really? What's his name?"

"Gordon."

"Gordon? Is he nice? Let's be honest."

Silence.

"You need someone who is nice. I know, because I don't have anyone who cares about me. If I had a chance to be with someone as nice as you I'd do anything you wanted. You can trust me. Honest."

Silence.

"You believe me, don't you? That you can trust me?"

"I guess."

"You could come and visit me, you know. I live all alone. I'm really lonesome. We'd get off at the next town."

"Sorry."

"You don't have to decide right away. We've got about twenty minutes till we get to my stop. Think about it. All I want you to do is smile. That nice big smile you have. I'd be so happy to have you with me. You're so young and so pretty. And you've got such a nice smile. I like to see it. You could get off when I do. Okay? We'll keep it a secret. I won't tell anyone."

"Sorry."

"Sorry? Does that mean no? Don't you like me? Not even a little bit? I'd be good to you. You'd see."

"No thanks. My folks are waiting for me at home."

"What about your boyfriend? Where's he?"

"I think I want to sit alone now."

"I'd really like you to come home with me. I'd be real good to you. You'd find out just how nice I can be."

"I think you should sit somewhere else now. Leave me alone."

"All right then. See? I'm going. I'm doing exactly what you said. But while you sit here all alone just think about it. Maybe you'll change your mind..."

"No."

"See how good I am to you? I'm leaving, just like you asked me. I'm going to look for an empty seat farther back. And I'll be getting off just as soon as this bus stops."

"Fine."

"Just give me a smile first and then I'll go. You're so sweet. And you've got such a beautiful smile."

Smoke

A WOMAN AT WORK is trying to give up smoking, doing it cold turkey: no patch, no chewing gum, no rewards. She almost inspires Megan to suffer, too. They could form their own support group: bargaining, consoling, distracting.

Megan finds smoking disgusting. For her, it's food.

The woman reminisces about old TV ads: *Winstons taste good like a* (three beats) *cigarette should.* And *L S M F T: Lucky Strike Means Fine Tobacco.*

Megan thinks she might just manage to eat healthy foods for a month. Four weeks plus a few days. Put that way it seems almost possible. And wouldn't you know it, what a nasty coincidence, a new month is just beginning, calling her bluff. The first of March. Unfortunately not the ides of. She'd have preferred a shorter month, but has just missed February, dammit. Perhaps she should wait until April, but by then the smoker would probably have begun puffing again.

Because the woman at work focuses on tobacco all the time. "Remember flat fifties? Fifty cigarettes in a sleek metal case? And remember that voice on TV, *"Players, please?"* She is nostalgic for those old days when life was simpler and every home had ashtrays, before cigarettes were banned from restaurants and offices and bars, from buses, streetcars, planes. "Remember elegant women smoking *Virginia Slims*? And there was a good-looking guy with an eye-patch that advertised some cigarette brand."

But Megan didn't pay attention to old TV ads, except the ones for food: *Kraft, Nabisco, Kellogg's....* "Remember that fruit bread from *Dominion* with icing on top?" she retaliates. "And remember *Honey Butter*? I think it was made by *McFeeter*." But the woman has no idea what Megan's talking about.

Such an important event as the start of a diet demands the dignity of a new month; it deserves at least that much recognition and respect, like a New Year's resolution, marking the beginning of something, and also the end, those Auld Lang Syne days. She is fifty-six years old already. Imagine! How many months is that anyway? Fifty-six times twelve. More than six hundred. Seven hundred, maybe. If she had a paper and pencil handy she could figure it out.

She thinks she ought to have become more cynical by now, should have learned not to find beginnings so hopeful. Turning over a new leaf, starting on a fresh slate, all those optimistic stale clichés. While ancient Father Time slashes his scythe at fields of old daydreams, making room for new ones.

Now Megan begins saving up tobacco stories to tell her. "A servant saw Sir Walter Raleigh smoking a pipe and thought he was on fire, so threw a bucket of water on him." Is this true, or has she just now made it up? She isn't sure, but then dredges up some more old memories. "Remember that old tobacco ad? A bellhop in a hotel lobby who kept calling for *Philip Morris*?"

It would be easier to diet if she took up smoking as a distraction. They could swap crutches, and later form a new two-person support group to help each other break their new addictions. Maybe she should suggest this. They could keep switching back and forth, faster and faster, like a silly skit on a late-night talk show.

But right now Megan is freezing. How come transit shelters are always designed wrong? Blasts of wind shove through the doorway and under the sides, swirling candy wrappers and newspapers and grit around her feet. Have the designers ever waited inside one? Or politicians? Probably not. They make too much money and use chauffeured limousines.

Megan tries to imagine a better design for a transit shelter but is too cold to concentrate.

Finally a streetcar is coming. Megan heads out of the shelter and watches it pass by without stopping.

"Did ya' see that?" A guy stops pacing outside the shelter and strikes up a conversation. "The way that driver went right past us? He shouldn't have done that. Especially on Sunday. He saw me waving my transfer. I don't care if he had a green light. He should have stopped and picked us up."

Megan always responds to strangers with just-right replies, not one word extra, then ending in closure. Polite though, polite and pleasant. "Sundays are different? Anyway, as if the transit system has rules."

This time it doesn't work.

"Yeah. Because on Sundays there aren't as many streetcars, so we'll have to wait longer for the next one."

"Right."

"I should have had the radio on, eh? And listened for a weather report."

"That's for sure." The guy's not even wearing a coat. He's massive, with a thick cushion of fat covering his chest and belly, so maybe he doesn't feel the cold. He's wearing a T-shirt, plus a sports shirt on top that is flopping open. Only one button fastened and Megan doesn't think it's in the matching buttonhole, but doesn't want to stare at him closely to find out.

The temperature has dropped again. Cold, ice-cold, gusty. News stations are probably quoting double temperatures: the actual cold, and whatever it feels like when the wind chill is factored in. But the numbers don't help Megan who never made the centigrade transition.

"I'm having pains in my chest."

Megan has trouble refocusing. "What? What? Chest pain? Do you have pills?"

"Yeah. They're at home. Nitro, right? You mean nitro?"

"Nitroglycerine pills. Yes." Two beats. "You don't keep them with you?" Thinking: You stupid bugger. If you just carried them like you're supposed to. If you wore a coat and kept them in the pocket.

He looks okay. Can he really be in pain? He seems just like an easy-going friendly guy who wants to talk.

Wow! Suddenly the heavy aroma surrounds them as a group of teenagers saunter past.

"Mary Jane," he says. "Did you notice?"

"Notice? If they had walked past any slower we'd be flying."

"I could get it," he says. "Medicinal. For arthritis pain. I qualify. There's a clinic. You don't even need a doctor's certificate if you're a senior."

He doesn't look old enough to be a senior. Maybe fifty, fifty-five max. "Really? Where is it?"

Now he pauses. Three beats. Wary. Perhaps wondering if he can trust her. "On Dundas. The north side. A couple of blocks west of Bathurst. That's all they do there. It's not free. You have to pay."

"But it's legal?"

"Yeah. I'm allowed to smoke it."

"Is it good for dieting? Maybe I should try it."

He laughs. "Doesn't help me."

He seems relaxed. The pain must have gone away.

Megan's mother doesn't get angina any more. She used to, years ago, and then it stopped. Why would this happen? But now she is terrified by something else, attacks of breathlessness. Sagging in the armchair this afternoon, gasping a little, her lungs grabbing for air. But she refused to sit still. "Come on. I want to show you something in the bedroom." Trying to shove herself up from her chair, grabbing at the walker.

"Never mind, Momma. I can see it later. Just sit and relax. Take it easy. Let your breathing settle down."

"Just keep sitting in this chair? That's all I do."

119

Not like Megan. She's got to get going, has places to go, people to meet, but her mother isn't ready to let go of her just yet. She yanks at the chain around her neck. "I hate wearing this thing. If I forget to take it off at night it gets tangled in my nightgown and wakes me up."

The necklace with an alarm button.

"No, Momma. You've got to wear it. Even at night. Especially at night! Dammit. You insist on living alone. Okay. I don't like it. Hate it, as a matter of fact. But at least I know you can call someone if you need to."

Silence.

"Right? You know that's what to do if you need help? Press that button?"

"What are you talking about? This thing here? No one ever told me."

Megan stares at this skinny woman who bears a faint family resemblance to her mother. This bony stranger.

Sigh. "I've told you, Momma. Lots of times. You've forgotten again."

Memory so temporary, evanescent as smoke.

Her mother can't get used to her body either and grabs at her skin. "Where did all these lumps come from? I always had nice smooth skin. I rub on lotion but they don't go away."

She has forgotten so much, but remembers having smooth skin.

"I can hardly see them," Megan lies, but it doesn't matter. Her mother can feel them and knows they're there.

It's time to leave. Megan hugs her mother goodbye. Gently, because the skin seems stretched so taut over her bones that it could crack apart at any moment. "Don't forget about the button. If you need help.... Or if you fall down...."

"Which button? You mean this thing?" She shakes the necklace. "Anyway, I don't care. I want to die. I'm tired of waiting. Why does God do this? Make me keep living on and on? I used to have so many friends but they kept dying. There's no one left."

Megan takes her coat off again. "It's not about dying, Momma. You don't need the button if you're dead. But what if you fall down and can't get up, can't reach the phone to call for help? You might be in pain. You would get hungry and thirsty, need to go to the bathroom."

"I need to go to the bathroom right now." She grabs the walker, lifts it up and carries it down the hall, so there won't be marks indented in the wall-to-wall carpet.

Megan is exasperated, fed up. "As if it matters," she complains later to the smoker at work. "As if anyone ever sees that carpet. As if Momma has visitors anymore except me and the woman from home-care," and the co-worker will remind her, as always, "*She* sees it. She's losing her memory, but still has her pride."

Yeah, right, Megan always thinks but never says. *Easy for you to say. You never bother visiting your own mother.*

Suddenly a streetcar arrives. It's not a mirage: the door is opening. She worries about the man having to climb up the steep stairs. "Are you still having pain?"

He is breathing hard and doesn't answer.

The car is crowded, but they find empty places and sit down quickly, gratefully, half a dozen seats apart.

Megan realizes she has become a creature of habit herself, falling into a comfortable pattern. Always making the same old complaints, even though she knows it's impossible for her mother to change. Her old habits probably keep her going; they are necessary, like Megan's junk food.

Suddenly she realizes the man is hollering at her. "I'm fine now," he yells, "ever since that lovely second-hand pot."

Maybe she has enough arthritis to qualify.

Thanksgiving Dinner

EVERYONE'S TALKING ABOUT last night's sitcom on TV. There's lots of time to discuss it while bowls and platters are passed around. Turkey. Mashed potatoes and mashed turnip. Green beans with cheese sauce. "Try some. I used three different kinds of cheese this time. See if you can guess which ones they are." Creamed cauliflower. Glazed carrots and onions. Cranberry sauce, sage and walnut stuffing, giblet gravy. They keep coming, one bowl after another, accompanied by encouraging comments: "Just try a spoonful of this," "Try some of that." Aunt Rita's bread and butter pickles. Aunt Charlotte's pickled watermelon rind. All mixed in with TV chatter. "I can't stand the new boyfriend on that sitcom. He never holds the door open for her."

"How about you, Almira? Do you get to watch that show? Does Baby Burton give you time out to watch the tube?"

"Maybe he will now. Guess what he found this week? He's got a new toy. He found his wiener."

"Oh, no!" says Grandma. "That's too bad. How did it happen?"

"Real easy, Granny. He just reached out and caught it, the same way he found his feet."

"You'll have to get his didies on faster."

"Well, my little sweetums likes having all his clothes off. I give him diaper breaks. He has sunbaths in his birthday suit by the kitchen window."

Aunt Rita speaks up. "Diaper breaks? What kind of foolishness is that? My Georgie never had bare-skin sunbaths. I hustled him into his clothes. Out of one layette set and into the next, quick, so he wouldn't catch cold. He never had a chance to play with himself."

Everyone looks at George. He brought his new girlfriend to this dinner and now regrets it.

Eugene says what everyone's thinking, "So, George, how old were you when you discovered yours?"

George studies the mashed turnips. "I don't remember."

George's girlfriend gets all huffy and leaves the room, but she's not gone long. "Where's the bathroom?" she stage-whispers near George's ear.

"Upstairs to the right," he tells her, "but Gramps is still in there. He takes a while."

She glares at George. "I'm in a hurry."

"Sorry, Sugar."

"Too bad you're not a guy," Charlene tells her. "They get to pee off the back porch. All those dandelions in the yard, they try to spray them like DDT."

"You're not supposed to know that, Charlene. You shouldn't look."

"I thought DDT was banned," says Esmerelda.

"Yeah, 'merelda. It was. That's why we pee them to death instead. It works. Those yellow tassel heads wither right up."

"Really?"

"Well, no, but we keep trying."

"You'll have to tie his wrists so he can't reach it," Grandma says. "That's what I did with my boys."

Everyone stares at the red faces of Uncle Roger and Uncle Herb and Uncle Virgil.

Uncle Virgil glares at Grandma. "Is that the truth? Are you serious? You tied our wrists?"

"You weren't so bad, Virgil," Grandma tells him. "Roger was worse."

Uncle Roger tries to deflect attention. "What about Herb, Momma? Didn't you tie him down, too?"

"Mind your own business," Uncle Herb hollers, trying to drown out Grandma's voice.

"No, I never tied Herb. I don't think he knew it was there."

But Uncle Virgil interrupts, "Anyway, what do you mean, you tied our wrists? Tied them to what?"

"The bed," Grandma explains. "I tied your hands to the sides of the bed."

"You mean we couldn't even turn over? We might have choked!"

"Well you didn't though, did you? You're all as healthy as halibut. Just look at you. Trying to argue while you're wolfing down turkey. You're more liable to choke right now."

"Take the baby's clothes off, Almira," Charlene suggests. "Let's see if he can find it again."

"No you don't, young lady," Grandma shrieks. "I'm in charge of what goes on around here. There's going to be no hanky-panky in my house."

"No hanky-panky. Hmm. Kinda makes you wonder how this family ever get started in the first place, don't it?" Uncle Roger directs his comment to Uncle Herb so he won't have to look Grandma in the eye.

Grandma's sputtering, "Now see here! There's no need for that kind of talk."

Just then Gramps returns. Grandma grabs his attention first. "Do something about the boys, Pa. Especially Roger. He needs a licking behind the woodshed."

"Too bad, Ma," Roger says. "Dad can't beat us up any more. He had to stop forty years ago when we grew big enough to hit back."

And now Grandma and the aunts start clearing the table and bringing in dessert.

Everyone else is watching Almira undress the baby. Baby Burton likes having his clothes off. He lies in her lap and coos.

Then he pees into the air. The little stream wavers toward the dinner table, mostly into a bowl of fruit cocktail, except for a few drops that land on the pumpkin pie. There is silence for a moment. Then Uncle Virgil murmurs, "Good shot, kid. Too bad there's no dandelions this time of year,"

Just then Grandma comes back from the kitchen bringing a serving spoon and a pie knife. "Well, now,' she says, "It's time for dessert." Then she remembers her manners and turns to George's girlfriend to serve her first.

Unborn Baby in Trailer Park

INALLY TRACY RETURNS, but Adam has moved the trailer to a different part of the RV park, and nothing seems familiar, including him. She has been back three days now, but he still seems like a stranger.

"Trying again," Adam calls this. Tracy doesn't call it anything. Naming makes it harder to let things go.

Luckily the aborted baby never had a name.

It keeps raining, day after day; no wonder Tracy and Adam are getting on each other's nerves. Rain drizzles down the trailer windows, and moisture condenses on the inside of the glass. The outside world has been softened to a gentle blur of green and grey. Tracy feels she is inside a cathedral, behind stained glass windows. She dreams she is a child again and still believes in a god she can pray to. Sleeping, she is able to dream she is secure.

Tracy knows this RV park's idiosyncrasies, and remembers the code to get into the shower room: 6-3-7. If she and Adam lived here with a child and watched it every minute the youngster would be safe. It couldn't shower until it was old enough to memorize the code, and tall enough to punch it in. So the toddler couldn't slip on a bar of soap, smash its head against the concrete floor, lie unconscious in the shower stall while warm water continued to spray down, until the child finally drowned.

However the door to the pool isn't locked. A child could

unlatch the gate, wander inside, reach out to touch the rippled flickering pattern on the water, then disappear inside its relentless embrace.

A security camera would record it; the coroner's jury could study the video tape.

The trailer park might offer Tracy and Adam a keepsake copy of the tape if they promise not to sue. They could buy a video recorder and watch the drowning happen, again and again, night after night. They could do this instead of making love.

Watching their child alive and happy, skipping to the edge of the pool, dabbling fingers into the water, then tumbling in. Bubbles rising toward the surface. Perhaps the toddler would come up for air three times before it drowned.

Adam's cat has eight extra lives, but the cat is safe here anyway; it can't open the door to the pool.

Tracy owns a dog now. She takes care of a husky pup instead of a baby. Things are tense inside the trailer, and the animals are one of the reasons why. Adam didn't know about the pup when he suggested they try again. Try for a relationship? Or try for another baby? Adam didn't specify and Tracy didn't ask. Anyway, not try for another abortion; neither of them wants to go through that again.

It is early morning. Tracy walks the pup along a path behind the trailer park. Beside them a bank slides down toward a dirty creek. It is peaceful. Inside their trailers people are still asleep. Except Adam. Tracy knows he lies awake, tense, waiting for her to return and climb back into bed.

Cars thrum along some highway in the distance. The highway is invisible. Perhaps it exists, she thinks. Perhaps she does.

Tracy keeps the pup on a leash. If it runs away she will have to stay in this trailer park until it comes back.

Eventually the pup will grow into a large devoted dog who will fiercely protect her, but right now it is young and friendly and wags its tail at strangers.

Like this man. He apparently slept beneath this railway

bridge. A campfire is smouldering. On the ground beside him is a backpack, with a hatchet looped through an outside strap.

The pup yelps, wags its tail, yanks Tracy toward the stranger.

Rain drizzles around them: Tracy, the pup, the man with the backpack hatchet.

"Hi," she says, because it is impossible not to speak. He is more formal and says, "Good morning." The dog nudges the man's crotch and sniffs, the way it does with other dogs, an awkward familiarity. A train roars above them on a trestle. Tracy wants to look up and count the cars as though she's still a carefree little kid.

Mist rises from the river and from the ground. People sleep peacefully inside their trailers. By now Adam has probably given up waiting, and fallen back to sleep.

Tracy and Adam sleep at the edges of the bed, as far away from each other as possible, leaving lots of space for the dead fetus that lies between them, its face as wrinkled as an old man's. Its eyes are always open; infants are curious and try to understand.

Tracy would like to understand things herself.

She believes in abortion, in choice, in wanted babies. She wasn't ready; Adam wasn't either. So why won't this fetus go away?

Once, at a party, somebody said, "Yuck. Family. They're the ones you don't pick," and everyone had laughed.

But there is a theory that infant souls select the parents they'll be born to. A lot of their hippie friends believe this kind of thing. Six months ago, a lifetime ago, she and Adam had laughed about it.

"Imagine me picking my parents," she had said, then made up a family from an article she'd read in a magazine. She described a fictional Prince Edward County childhood: the week-long heritage celebrations, her parents wearing pioneer costumes in the parade, her father carrying an old Loyalist flag, the cross of St. George. Then Adam tried to one-up her.

"Imagine me picking mine," and told tales of the Rosedale aunts and nannies who had raised him. Perhaps his story was true; Tracy has no way of knowing. They have never met each other's families, so can make up whatever they want. No one will contradict them.

If only they had been able to select ideal parents, then their lives together might have fallen neatly into place. Everything would be perfect between them now.

Like it once was. Because Tracy and Adam share the memory of a relationship that once seemed ideal. "As though we were made for each other," they'd kept saying.

Perhaps that's all we could hope for, Tracy thinks. Perhaps the memory of past happiness should be enough.

Once Tracy wanted a baby, then changed her mind. Now she wants another, but doesn't want to sleep with some guy in order to get it. Not even Adam. But she wants a child soon, before she gets any older, while she is thirty, (where did the time go?), and still energetic. She can imagine raising a child for the next twenty years, but could she commit to living with its father? Adam? A constant reminder of the abortion? She's not sure.

She has read about artificial insemination by donor, feeling a bit repulsed, yet fascinated; but now she wonders what kind of men would volunteer. Perhaps in some of these trailers, behind closed blinds, men are shooting sperm into jars that once contained marmalade or instant coffee.

Unborn infant searches for perfect parents. It watches men jerk off in jam jars. It watches Tracy shop for whole grain bread, green vegetables, alfalfa sprouts, and nods in approval.

Unborn baby checks the shopping cart of a prospective father: frozen fish sticks, frozen meat pies, frozen waffles and ice cream. This is a man who would put his sperm on ice if someone asked him. But Tracy could change his eating habits, feed him salads, lentils, unpolished rice. The man waits for someone to care enough to do this. Tracy's shopping cart collides with that of the prospective father, but she's checking expiry dates and doesn't notice.

Then Tracy returns to the trailer park. Unborn baby didn't expect this. It can imagine fishing and camping with Adam, tossing a softball back and forth, all the cliché father activities, but it worries about that earlier abortion. What if these two still don't feel ready? Unborn baby isn't sure whether to risk it.

Maybe it doesn't matter. Unborn baby watches Tracy, the husky pup and the man with the knapsack hatchet, and wonders whether a murder is about to happen.

Apparently not. The moment passes. The pup sees a chipmunk on the path and yanks Tracy toward it. They enter the trailer park from a different direction and never see the man again.

Inside the trailer Adam is half asleep, but he reaches for Tracy as she climbs into bed, and she slides into his arms as though she still fits there. And now, although they don't know it, they are beginning another baby. By the time Tracy discovers this she will have already moved on. She decides to raise the baby by herself and doesn't want Adam to ever find out.

Tracy never knew her own father so she's sure her child will get along just fine without one.

A Woman Wakes Up
in the Morning

A WOMAN WAKES UP in the morning and remembers her name. By the time she finds a pen and paper the name is lost.

She wakes up every morning. It happens so often that she gets used to it. She doesn't practise how to sit up, open her eyes, grumble, "Oh no! It's morning already!" All these things become a habit. An alarm rings: she turns it off, yawns, stretches, rubs her eyes, thinks the sun will be shining or it will not. She glances at the window and sees that one of these is true. Her days become predictable. She blames the patterned mornings that begin them, and tries to change these, but is unable.

The woman wakes up and wonders whether she's awake. She wakens from a dream of waking from a dream, and so on.

She goes out to get her hair cut. Mirrors cover the opposite walls of the shop. She watches her reflections get smaller, then disappear. Alice ate a piece of cake and shrunk smaller and smaller. Where will it all end, the woman wonders, and Alice wondered. The woman never enters that hair salon again. She lets her hair grow and tries to believe she's strong like Samson. The woman wakes up every tangled morning of her life.

An infant wakes up outside the womb and can't believe it. A perfect amniotic world burst apart, then disappeared. The baby keeps trying to forget this ever happened.

A toddler wakes up screaming. The room lights up. A face grows larger and makes sounds. Arms reach out and grab. The

131

131

child always remembers that sensation: the bed slipping away, the sudden approach of ceiling.

A teenager wakes up, music fastened by earphones to a syncopated brain. Feet already dancing. Fingers drumming a windowsill, wash-basin, kitchen table. Feet bopping out the door. Look out world! Here is someone who plans to nudge you, nudge you, nudge you until you dance.

A woman wakes up and remembers how much there is to do. She pretends she's still asleep. She sleepwalks as she makes breakfast; fights with children over boots, snowsuits, mittens, toques; is silent with a husband who won't be home for dinner. She rides a bus, waits on tables, tries to forget. On weekends she bakes cookies for Little Red Riding Hoods to take to Grandma.

An old woman wakes up, stares out a window. She remembers being anyone: Goldilocks, Little Red Riding Hood, Little Red Riding Hood's mother. Finally she looks in a mirror. She can't avoid it any longer. Oh no! Somehow she turned into Silverlocks when she wasn't looking. A bear or wolf or something waits to eat her up. She plans to walk into the forest and meet it halfway.

A woman wakes up in the morning. She might as well.

Acknowledgements

The following stories were previously published:

"The Keel Lies Underneath the Water with the Fish," *Zymergy* 4.2 (1990); and in *Best Canadian Stories* (Oberon Press, 1991).

"Bad Men Who Love Jesus at the Last Minute," *New Quarterly* 8 (2003).

"In Bed Beside a Stranger," *Grain* 22.2 (1994).

"Bruise-Woman," *Crash* 2 (1992).

"Dawn," *New Quarterly* 20.3 (2001).

"Neighbours," *Vivid: Stories by Five Women* (Mercury Press, 1989).

Carol Malyon has worked as a nurse, and then in health research, before owning a bookstore and hosting a reading series in the Toronto's beaches area. She has published the poetry collections, *Headstand; Emma's Dead;* and *Colville's People;* the short story collections, *The Edge of the World* and *Lovers and Other Strangers;* and the novels, *If I Knew I'd Tell You; The Adultery Handbook; The Migration of Butterflies;* and *Cathedral Women;* and a children's picture book, *Mixed-up Grandmas.* She and bill bissett co-authored *Griddle Talk,* a year of conversations at the Golden Griddle, where they discussed "love and life and anything else you want." She is based in Toronto, but has led short story workshops in the Maritimes and North Bay, and has been writer-in-residence at the University of New Brunswick. www.carolmalyon.com